Journey of Grace

Olwyn Harris

Reading Stones Publishing

Stock image provided by Shutterstock: www.shutterstock.com
Cover models are AI generated images courtesy of Canva.com

Published by: Reading Stones Publishing
Helen Brown; and Wendy Wood

Cover Design: Wendiilou Designs
           Wendy Wood

For more copies contact the publisher at:
Glenburnie Homestead
212 Glenburnie Road
ROB ROY NSW 2360
Mobile: 0422 577 663
Email: Readingstonespublishing@gmail.com

To the women who have allowed me to journey with them through all sorts of hard times...

Dellaweir

1883

* * *

There was a disciple named Tabitha,
"Gazelle" in our language.
She was well-known for doing good and helping out.
They showed pieces of clothing
the Gazelle had made while she was with them.
(Acts 9:36, 39 The Message)

Prologue

The wagon dragged slowly over the rough track. Nothing was right. The sun was hot; flies buzzed relentlessly around her head from the flanks of the bullocks in front. The landscape was brown and dry, ugly, harsh. That was all she could think. *This* was the opportunity, the fresh start, the do-over, the dream of a better life? Well, nothing was better. It was all worse. Every part of it. She pulled her tattered shawl around her shoulders and wondered how she had ever conceived that this could have been a better thing to do. It wasn't at all.

But better was no longer part of her reckoning. Now it was just about survival. Getting by in a land that was as barren as the dreams she once cherished. She had thought her other life was desolate. She hated it so passionately. She despised its predicable tyranny. But she knew nothing! She realised now, oh yes, it had been hard, but it had been doable. Fleetingly she thought of the day she walked up that gangplank with a ticket and a dream and a laugh on her lips. How unbelievably naïve! She wished she could go back and warn that girl; tell that smiling child of a woman to stay behind... to live out her days, hard and worn, but alive, and cold, and predicable. Nothing about this place was benevolent. It was stifling hot, and it felt like death.

They stopped in the middle of the track. A spindly sort of tree and some shrubby bushes was all that offered respite from the sun. The driver lifted down his water bag and slurped a drink. He passed the canvas over to his off sider who guzzled and swiped his mouth with the back of his hand. Tabitha stared at him, her lips cracked and dry. "You want some of this don't ya?" he said. She looked away.

Her travelling companion was a woman who went by the name of Alphie. She was buxom and bold, and although she was younger than Tabitha, she had all the appearances of being as wise in the matters of the world as any woman twice her age. Alphie jumped down from the dray and sidled over to him. She whispered something in his ear, and he smirked. He handed her a drink and she made eyes at him while drinking her fill.

Tibby looked away. Her thirst would not kill her yet. The pair scampered away into the sparse scrubland; Alphie giggling and hooting as they went. Tabitha gagged. Nothing about this was appropriate. The woman was going to meet her husband. The scrub was hardly dense enough to be modest. She turned away and tried to block out the noises.

Suddenly, the wagon driver dragged at her shawl, and she was caught off balance.

"Seems like it's time for you to pay ya passage as well. Always a good idea to try out the brides to see if they're up for the ride," he said crassly, his speech sprinkled with profanities.

Tabitha gasped and let out a yelp. "Get your hands off me! I've paid my fare!"

"Well, ain't you a fine and dandy one? All too good for us common folk? Well, I can show you I'm just as good as youse." He pulled her roughly, barely beyond the track, before he pushed her to the ground. She scrambled to her feet, but was hauled in by his great hairy paw, and he clouted her across the face. She fell down, hitting her head hard, dazed by terror. She screamed out and was silenced by another blow to her jaw. Pain screeched through her head. Eyes. Go for the eyes... but her body was pinned and buckled in searing pain, again and again. And when she thought it was over, she saw the leering teeth of his off sider above her and she blacked out as he hit her and it started again.

Tabitha was barely aware of the sway of the dray. Once or twice, they tried to sit her up, but she vomited and collapsed, blood oozing from her mouth and a gash in her head. Agitated voices buzzed as she rattled and vibrated over the track.

Somewhere voices were echoing in the distance. "But she's a Bates' whore..."

"Hell, we can't give her to Bates looking like this..."

"Ain't our fault she's got no spark. Who knew she'd look like she'd been dragged through a stampede? That ain't our fault!"

"You're right. But we got to come up with something before we get there, or this'll be our last delivery."

"Ain't known Bates to be that fussy as long as they can stand and walk."

"Wrap her up tight and we'll dump her off at the next joint. We'll be well gone by the time they figure it out. Bates won't be doing no swapping back once he meets this other little butter-nut. We'll tell the other guy that his bolted. And she would of... if truth-be-known."

With the finesse of branding scrubber yearlings, they bundled her up in bags like a roll of carpet and, without pausing, dumped her off the back of the dray. Her two small carry bags hit the dust beside her in the clearing that belonged to Zachary Logan, along with the couple of bags of his supplies.

2.

Zachary spent a little extra time down at the lagoon that afternoon. He was thinking about something more often than usual. Rupert Bates was his neighbour across the creek; he'd order women from an agency for his men. It seemed like bidding for a breeder from the stock yards. A string of bad luck had hit them though. One died of dysentery – at least that was what was said. Another got caught in a dray wheel. One of the others wandered off and got lost in the bush and was never found. Bolted probably. Bates' own wife died in childbirth. Rupert Bates was a thickset man with a thick set of hands, and he seemed to attract men of a similar ilk. Zach shook his head and was glad it was not for him to judge.

There was prestige in the offer Bates gave his men: the opportunity of a bride. It was a huge incentive. Hence, he imported them, brides who were encouraged to take a position with settlers. The altruism that seemed to endorse motherland family values was more about a bed and a meal at least once a day. He wondered how desperate a woman would need to be to try that on for size. Just a legal form of slavery in his mind and just because a woman held the keys, it didn't make it less of a prison. Rupert's aunt, Mrs Novak, had arrived to support Rupert's wife during her confinement and labour... and then never left after the small, private funeral. Everyone knew Mrs Novak reigned with tough seniority at Redlands Park.

Zach looked at the sun, gathered his shirt and hitched up his braces over his shoulders. He whistled to his dog, "Hey Skitter", as he walked back to his hut. He paused at the back door and looked around. Even for a bachelor it was sparse. Everything that had been so satisfactory yesterday now seemed beyond inadequate. He should make some furniture, like a proper hutch, just to make it a little friendlier. He went outside to set the fire in his lean-to kitchen. He found a mug and plate, rinsed them in a wooden pail and started readying his dinner. Zachary was not one to do things in a hurry, but he resolved then, that at least some improvements were necessary. And he figured that if he didn't strike while the iron was hot, he'd be still thinking about it when he was greying around his sideburns and getting stiff in the joints.

He opened the front door and stood on his little verandah looking down the track towards the road that came from town. Supplies were due today. He shaded his eyes against the glare and looked at the horizon. Going to be hot tomorrow.

Skitter ran out and disappeared down the track. Zachary looked at the setting sun and realised the deliveries probably had already been dropped off. Typically, they were dumped by the track near the road, with various degrees of carelessness. He hitched his billycart with his goat, Bob, and led him down to gather the supplies. But irritation turned to curiosity, changing to a weird feeling of disbelief, as he spotted Skitter sniffing and whining over a long bundle lying beside the bags.

His heart pounded with dread as he turned it over. He was sure her limp body was dead. He felt for her breath on his cheek, and quickly lifted her up onto the billycart and led Bob back to the hut. He peeled off the hessian bags and carried her inside, laying her on his stretcher. Her over-heated body was swollen with bruises. He was relieved to hear her moan. He grabbed a drink of water from the pail outside and lifted it to her lips. Most of it dribbled to the side, but slowly she swallowed.

He grabbed a rag, and a basin and poured water over her to cool her hot, dry, dehydrated skin. He wiped the crusted blood from her lips, a grim look forming in his eyes. He paused for a second and wondered how far he could go. But he had nursed sick animals, and he figured he would not do less for a person. He removed her tattered shawl and torn blouse and pinafore and found a clean loose shirt of his own from behind his door. He washed her over, and as he soothed the bruises and blood on her thighs, a deep-seated rage boiled inside of him. He had never felt so wild, and yet so constrained to be gentle. He fanned her modestly covered body and held her head for another drink.

He retrieved her canvas bag with his supplies from the cart. He laid her things on the floor. There was an envelope. Zachary looked at it bewildered. Where did this woman come from? Why was she here? Who did this to her?

He offered another drink. He pulled one of the squatter's chairs over beside the bed, stood a box on its end and positioned the lamp on it. Then he settled in for the night. Slowly, slowly. He would rehydrate her the only way he knew how: one thimbleful at a time.

Zachary rubbed his forehead as he looked at the bed from his chair. He needed help, he knew that, but he couldn't leave. Wouldn't. Over the years, whenever Zach was backed into a corner, he'd stiffen his back and defend his position. This was no different. He had to do what he could, but a niggly doubt wondered if this wouldn't spring back and bite him. What were the chances he'd be accused of her death if she didn't pull through? Who else knew she was here? Who was she? Surely someone would miss her?

Another thimbleful of water. And another. He rung out the wet rag and wiped it across her forehead again. Again and again, at regular intervals, like drip-feeding an orphaned lamb, he worked through the dark.

Somewhere between the first streaks of dawn and the sun rising, he dozed off. He was jolted awake by a weak cough. Instinctively he reached for the water, and this time she swallowed more intentionally. He made a syrupy concoction from wild honey. He boiled wallaby meat and strained the broth through a rag. He locked the calf away from his mother overnight and milked the cow in the morning. He never bothered with the milk for himself, but this seemed a better cause. The first day... then the next... and then the next. She said nothing, except delirious moaning, or vague assents of compliance or groans of objection. After a week she was sitting out of bed in a chair for meals, very slowly taking the soft foods he prepared.

He looked at her as she stirred awake and there was clarity in her eyes. "Good mornin'", he said as he stretched, stiff from his vigil. "I'm reckoning on a cup of tea. Had planned that the first day you came, but seems you were not up to it then." Her eyes followed him, suspicious and uncertain, as he left the room.

He came in with two mugs and set them on the box. He helped her sit up in bed, and he handed her the drink. "Not sure how

much you remember. My name is Zach. This is my place –
Dellaweir. Means 'Noble Watering-hole'. I've been living here nigh
eight years, I'm guessing. You've been here about eight days. What's
your name?"

"Tabitha."

"Tabitha..." He repeated the sound of it. "So, you remember
then." He liked the idea that she had a name. More than once he had
this sinking feeling she may not remember, may not want to
remember. But she did. Her name at least.

"Tabitha. Tabitha Francis Flanders. My brothers and sister
called me Tibby. I'm from Lancashire."

"Oh." He paused, thinking of something he had not thought
of for a very long time. "How'd you get here?"

"Boat. I had assisted passage. Three months. The trip wasn't
a lot of fun."

He hadn't meant that, but he allowed her the dignity to dodge
his question. He wanted to know: was someone waiting for her...
worried about her. "I'm wondering who might be missing you," he
said as he got up and brought the envelope over to the bed. He
paused. He had to ask. "Do you read?" he asked apologetically.

She nodded. "A bit."

"Does it say where you were supposed to be going?"

She opened the envelope and looked at the paper, cringing.
Like seeing through a haze, she remembered. Winnie had been so
convincing. This was to be their ticket to security.

"You are...?"

"Just a farmer."

"No, your name."

"Oh. Zach. Zachary Logan."

"Oh." She concentrated hard on the document trying to make sense of it. Her eyes would hardly focus. "The name I had was B... Banes, or Bratts... Robert... perhaps."

He stared at her. "Bates? Rupert Bates? You were supposed to go there?"

The sharpness in his tone shocked her, but he stood up and opened the shutters. Tabitha turned the page: details of passage arrangements. Suddenly she went cold. And pale. She leaned over and grabbed a bowl and was sick. "I don't remember," she said, and she pushed it away.

"Just rest. I'll make breakfast. We'll talk more later."

She noticed how he respected her modesty as he handed her the shawl. Who was he? Why did he keep showing up with drinks and offers of food?

Zachary went and chopped some wood, allowing his disgust to surge through the axe. This woman was headed for Bates? He saw her eyes shroud in fear. The cuts on her lips were healing. He felt some relief as the wood blocks split and catapulted away. He didn't retrieve them. He had enough wood under the lean-to that kept the weather out. Without actually saying 'murder' he was certain she would not be holding an enamel mug just now, if fate had not dumped her at his gate. Another block split.

He had thought a fair bit about God since he decided to take charge of his destiny and come here. Aloneness has a way of driving one into the hands of Our Maker. He had asked for divine intervention. Was this it? Somehow it felt like this tragedy was being retrieved back from the brink of hell. He positioned another block and split it hard down the middle. His hand was already dealt. He split another and determined this was a hand he was ready to work with. As he traced her face during through those long nights of fevers, something had locked in. He knew when something felt right. And this felt like it was meant to be. It was time to have the whole deal... not just a bride paid to be here, but a wife who loved back.

3.

Zach went out to the woodheap and left her to attend to her ablutions at the very crude washstand: a wooden pail perched on a box. A small cloth and a larger rag sufficed as the toiletry linen. He stood looking down the scrub track that led to the creek. He was uncomfortable with inactivity. He was used to moving. Cutting a tree, building a fence, butchering his meat, burning his dinner. It didn't even seem to matter whether it was constructive movement or not, but the act of motion seemed to generate within him the sense of advancement. Motion he did, but granted, he knew it was usually not quick. Others might look at him and see stagnation and complacency, but when Zach knew what he was aiming for, he was dogged in his persistence.

He started hewing wood again. Even when he built the main hut, his stack of hewn logs was never high. Repetitive motion. He put down his adze and slid another squared log onto the pile that was held in place between a couple of trees used as his timber-rack.

He heard a gentle cough behind him and spun around. Tabitha was standing there in a plain, rather worn dress. The frayed seams on her clean apron were soft and seemed to glow. He averted his eyes, embarrassed.

Tibby saw him look away and felt an overwhelming sense of shame. She stood with downcast eyes.

Zachary wished he could be bolder. "Do you need something?" He cringed. Clumsy. Would she prefer one of those smooth confident men from town? Suave, composed, confident. But this was him. Plain. Simple. Uncomplicated.

She stopped. "Oh. Umm. I don't think so. I wanted to thank you for looking after me. And I ... ahh... wondered... how much I owe. I only have a little to pay with."

He turned to her then; curiosity squelching any qualms he had. He noticed her bashful look, her neck flushing red. "Payment? I didn't expect any. In fact, I figured... purely an assumption on my part I suppose... that any woman with independent means wouldn't choose to be an immigrant bride."

"Do you not believe in marriage, Mr Logan?" Perhaps he didn't. There was no evidence of a woman, no indication that this was on his mind.

That she would censure him with lack of interest struck him as ironic. He was quickly becoming very enamoured with the idea. "It's not something that has been... well, as you can see... a priority. Dellaweir is very much a bachelor's place. Umm..." He wondered how to proceed. "You asked if you owed me. No. Nothing. But..." He paused. He needed a plan. He had the formation of one, but he wasn't sure how to articulate it.

"But...?" Of course, he would object to her being here. That was unseemly... immoral.

"I was thinking... that you need to be stronger before you tackle the road... if that is still your intention."

"I probably should follow up the contact I was given."

Oh. So, she was determined to go on with the plan. Well, he didn't want her feeling indebted. "Okay then. Umm... it's just that I need help with something, and I was wondering... if you might help out? It could be for board and lodging... until you feel well enough to travel of course."

Fear jumped into her eyes. Would he also demand payment for services rendered? Perhaps she should just run for it.

He saw her face pale, and her body tremble. "Oh please, sit down before you fall down," he said and moved a block of wood into the shade and retrieved a mug of water. She sat without taking the drink. He propped it on another stump and sat opposite her... away. He hoped it was a respectful distance.

"You see... you make a valid point, I think. This is not a place for a woman. Having you here makes that obvious. But... well... I..." He paused and wondered how he could do this. "I... am... umm... I'm expecting a lady visitor. And I need to fix up the place before I can even consider she might stay. I've got no idea about these things, and it's kinda timely for you to be here. I wondered if you would advise me... on how to go about that."

She looked up at him. Not as a desolate man, a little creepy around the fringes in his isolation... but as a man with a fiancé or beloved kinfolk separated by distance. Someone who was loved... and loving. It explained his cautious reserve, his awkward yet gentle care. "Your lady friend... is she your 'intended' then?"

"Umm..."

She smiled at his confusion. "You must know if you plan to marry?"

He shook his head. "She is not my fiancé... but family. In fact,..." He swallowed. "...she is my sister."

Ah. Beloved kinsfolk. "What is your sister's name?"

He faulted and cleared his throat. "Heather."

"Is she married?"

"Well no. Widowed actually. But I think she is betrothed again. When she comes, I would like her to be comfortable. I'm not sure how long she will stay..."

Tabitha smiled and stood up. She took his arm as they walked back inside. A family that was different to her messy, cluttered, rough, unruly family sounded appealing. "What would you like me to do?"

"Well, I'm not sure. I mean... to start with, I've been thinking if you are going to stay... while you get stronger of course... it would be proper to have a separate room. Now that you are okay, I need a different set up. I'll still use my swag until I get a bed sorted." He walked over to the window. "What do you think about making a bedroom through here? I'll need another room anyway, and if we do that first, you will be comfortable... while you're here..." A thought passed through his mind that if she didn't get stronger, she wouldn't have to leave. Then he reprimanded himself for not being sensible. Sensible had been Zach's foremost rule about everything.

"You're going to build a room... by yourself?"

"Sure. I built the hut. I think that would be the best place, don't you?"

She realised he was actually asking her. That felt strange. She watched him pace out a distance and hammer in a stake on the corners of the proposed space.

"Umm... you want me to help you to build this?" She wasn't sure she'd manage a construction job.

"Well, maybe hold something now and then. It's really the women's stuff I don't get. I know I need a bed... but what else?"

Tibby listed a few items off the top of her head. "... table linen and draperies... bed sheets and a quilt."

"Oh. See. Now I am lost." He grinned at her. "I think you will make a good advisor in matters domestic."

Tabitha blushed. "I can sew some. If you had fabric, I could start some of those things for you. It will give me something to do... if you wouldn't mind, of course..."

"Not at all. There are other things I need from town. Write me a list, and I'll give it to the Haberdashery shop, when I go in." It seemed his mind was set. "What else?"

Nothing else. She just needed to be better and get on with her life. She was grateful for the distraction this project would offer while she did that.

4.

Tibby woke up, the lumps in the straw-filled tick mattress were familiar to the aches in her body. She stretched, wincing, her bruises still tender. She stared at the vertical streams of morning light through the cracks between the slabs that made up the wall of the hut, playing with the dust in the air. Morning. It was strange how quickly she was learning to appreciate dawn, rather than dread another terrible day ahead. Already she found comfort in the routines here. Ablutions. Breakfast. A little light housekeeping; then some laundry. Meal preparations. Reading. Zach liked her to read after dinner when they would sit and talk for a while. He only had a Bible, but he didn't seem to mind the lack of literary diversity. Her stamina was not strong so everything she did was in small, regulated stints. Rest was imperative. Her body demanded it.

She lay there, contented, as she listened for the sounds of the house. Zach was always up when she woke. He was not a quiet worker and had this constant muffled self-dialogue that accompanied whatever he did. But just now, she was greeted by silence. Silence. As she became aware of it, the silence became louder. She looked over at the squatter's chair and the swag in the corner. They stood empty. Skitter lay on his hessian bag beside it with his head on his forelegs. She listened for wood chopping, billy rattling, fire crackling. It was stony quiet. A magpie warbled in the scrub, but its music did nothing to reassure her. Maybe he was down by the creek collecting water. She got out of bed and opened the door. She could see his goat, Bob, eating some leaves off a low shrub. The water cart was left undisturbed by the shed. Skitter came and stood by her side, and she reached down and rubbed his ears. Dew rested on everything. There were no boot-prints, marking the steps of morning traffic... even to the bushes.

She turned back confused. She hung onto the door jamb, dazed. Her breathing became raspy, and her chest pounded. She felt giddy. She wanted to scream, but she couldn't. Her breath seemed to strangle any sound from her. She desperately wanted to get out, away, but her body refused to move. She stood paralysed: alone, exposed, vulnerable. Sweating, she stumbled over to Zach's squatter chair, knocking a pitcher of water to the floor. She climbed into the chair, curled herself up small and pulled the grey blanket off his swag up over her head. She couldn't breathe, and she didn't care. If she blacked out it might stop. But she didn't black out... and it didn't stop. It went on and on and on. She felt Skitter's nose on her arm, and he edged into the chair and huddled beside her. She wrapped her arm around his body, and he licked the tears from her face. Slowly, slowly her breathing regulated to his... and she finally submitted to her exhaustion.

She stirred in the dimness as Skitter wriggled from her hold and bounded to the door. Her panic started to rise again as the door latch rustled. "Hey, Skitter... been a long day..." She stared at the face of the man standing in the door trying to recognise who it was. He lit a lamp and scanned the room from the unmade bunk, the turned over water pitcher that had leaked through the floorboards, over to her haggard face and sweat stained hair; dog-hair on her night-dress; his blanket wrapped around her.

Zach leaned his saddle up against the wall. He came over and hunched down in front of the chair. "Tibby?"

Tears streamed down her face as he reached out. He helped her stand and she wavered; her frame shuddered with sobs. She screamed then. All the screams that refused to come before, now came, and came and came, and she hit, and she kicked, and she flailed.

He recognised this. It reminded him of a small, skittish, dust-covered pup he'd picked up from the track, as it yelped and bit and cowered. It had taken a while but Skitter was his inseparable mate now. Zach held her against him, bracing himself against the feeble, angry onslaught. Her shaking arms slowing until they had no more motion. He held her and steered her towards her bunk, pulled back the covers, and supporting her back against the pillow.

He said nothing, but he laid down beside her, on top of the covers, wrapping his strong arms gently around her, as she sobbed herself to sleep. His mind slowing to a patient, determined pace. It was something of a gift in his makeup. He understood he had a way of restoring health. Skitter hadn't been the only one. His horse had been a scrawny worm-ridden filly that the owner sold for a pittance just to save the bullet it would require to put her down. His ewe had also been a bedraggled, unfortunate looking beast. He was really after the wool, and maybe some mutton stew down the track, but when she happened to be in lamb, he nurtured the mother, who was able to nurture her lamb as well. He started his herd with some rather ordinary cows, but he had made a solid investment in a good stock bull. This was familiar territory. He was not afraid of this at all. The only difference was... this time it was different; completely different.

4·

Tibby woke and she lay there, feeling the lumps in the straw-filled tick mattress familiar under her weight. She stretched her muscles, cramped and aching, the bruises across her arms pained. She opened her eyes. The swag beside squatter's chair in the corner, and Skitter's hessian mat beside it, were empty. She listened anxiously and her breathing quickened. A magpie warbled in the scrub. Then she heard the wood chopping, billy rattling, fire crackling. But it was the muffled voice of Zach muttering away to his dog that reassured her most... and she breathed easy. She climbed stiffly out of bed and opened the back door. Zach looked up from over the fire. "Morning. Fixing a cuppa."

"I'm starving. I could eat a horse." She flushed with embarrassment.

He grinned with approval. "Well, we are particularly lucky to have honey this morning. Damper coming up." They licked and slurped their way through slabs of it.

After breakfast, Zach pointed out a pile of packages on the rough logs that ran along the wall in a crude shelf. "They are for you."

"Me?"

"Yeah... got them yesterday."

"Yesterday?" The horror of yesterday sent a cold shiver down her spine. She stared at him as he brought over a bundle of brown paper packages.

"Yeah. Didn't come back with just honey."

"I woke up and you were gone," she said, her face tight.

"I said I was going to get you material." Did she doubt he was a man of his word? Or was she just plain vague?

"You said you *might* if I made a list. I didn't make a list."

"Huh." Zach felt his equilibrium tilt. He shouldn't have to explain what he was doing or where he was going. He'd had eight independent years of not having to explain anything to anyone. Eight years, though, when no one missed him; he kind of liked the idea he was missed. "Anyways, you said you might try some sewing."

Tabitha stared at him. No apology. No explanation. And as the moment extended it became obvious to her that he didn't care. She knew Zach well enough to know he would never intentionally hurt her, but she had thought he cared. The chasm of being abandoned was so overwhelming yesterday. That wasn't too different from what she felt now. She stared at him standing there in the morning light as if nothing was different. She impatiently took one of the packages and unwrapped it. She turned over the bolts of plain-weave cloth in despair. "You got *this* to make your house more homely?"

Zach shrugged. "The bloke at the shop said it was versatile."

"Maybe... but... well, this is like dressing your stuff in hessian. Calico is hardly going to create a homely place for your sister."

"What?"

"Heather: your sister. We were getting ready for her visit."

"Oh. Yes." It never even occurred to him that he could get fabric wrong, or that she would have definite notions about appropriate homemaking. "Guess that sort of proves my point; I don't have a clue about these female matters. But it's what we have now, so you'll have to use it."

"At least there is enough here to do just about everything," she said dubiously. Would he blame her if this did not work out? Her mistress had complained of customers who wanted a silk purse made out of a pig's ear. *"Conjurers they want... not a seamstress!"*

"The shop guy... was he right? Is it functional?" If he had been sold useless stuff, that would be a waste. He wasn't one for waste.

Tibby sighed and tried not to be disappointed. She smoothed the frown on her forehead and nodded. "Yep, it's functional. Not sure it will be homely though." She had been intrigued by the offer – the opportunity to create 'homely'. But now, all she had to work with was functional. When you are cold, even newspaper is functional. She knew that well enough... but she wanted to believe a home, a real home, that could be more than just functional. *Homely.*

"Well, it'll do the job. Nothing wrong with practical." He spoke tersely.

"I thought the idea was also having a woman's perspective!"

He felt that pang of prickly again. What right did she have to be annoyed with his best efforts? "I figured I should keep that woman's thing under my hat. They'd get the wrong idea – you being here. Practical won't raise any eyebrows."

"Well... I'll think about it some. I'm sure we can do something for your sister that is not going to have this place looking like a barn."

He looked out the bare window where the shutters were propped open. He had not heard the term "we" used like that. It sounded normal and strange and awkward and oddly intimate, and he abruptly went outside and picked up his adze. He went back to the task of dressing more logs, preparing them for building.

Tibby didn't even know where to start. This plain-weave was like looking at a dirty cobble street after anticipating the relief of lush pasture. She had once seen a painting of sheep on a hillside of verdant meadowlands. That painting hung in a wide polished framed, featured in the parlour of a lady who had not been home when she made a delivery. The maid had given Tibby a peek at life on the other side... the top side. That painting captured her imagination and she had wondered for weeks what meadows and meadows of deep green grass might feel like under her running feet.

She sat on the verandah staring at the vast layers of textured brown that collaged the Australian bush paddocks before her. She thought of the textile factories surrounded by miles of rusty-red brick and mortar and cluttered streets, that were another world away. There had been no soft edges in that drab landscape where she grew up. Just sharp angles of buildings. Here, there was a different sort of harshness: jagged rocks and severe escarpments of the scrubby stiff trees, the long spear shaped leaves. If she hoped Australia might be different, it certainly was. More different than she could ever imagine. It was proud and rough and determined, mocking her naïve romanticism that desired lush, and soft, and homely. The landscape before her seemed to go on forever in a hundred shades of brown like a sepia photograph. How ironic that grass was bleached to the colour of calico.

Tibby went out to where Zach was hewing logs. He stopped to stretch and ran his arm up over his forehead where his hair flopped in his eyes. The physical work had settled him some.

She stood awkwardly for a moment and then blurted out, "I'm sorry. I don't want to fight."

"Oh. I thought we were talking."

"Talking?"

"Yeah. Talking. You don't like the plain weave. I was disappointed I let you down. I don't see it as fighting just because we see things different."

"Oh." She hadn't thought about it like that.

"Well. What would be the point on having you consult if I already had the same ideas? I wouldn't need your point of view at all."

"Oh."

"And last night... when I got in, you were so messed up, I didn't even think you'd be up for talking at all today... so I am pleased you feel you can."

"What do you mean?"

"Last night... when I came in... you were... It took a while before you settled. I stayed with you till you went to sleep..." He looked at her mystified look on her face. "You don't remember that? You crying... me holding you...?"

"You were there?"

"Of course. I don't want you to be scared, Tibby. You are safe here. I want you to know that."

"Oh. I thought you... well, I know you wouldn't hurt me of course... but I thought you... just left me to it... and I felt... it felt so alone all day."

"Well, I've been doing alone for a long time now, so this is new to me. I won't always get it right. I know that. But I wouldn't just up and out when you are like that. Perhaps I need some advising on how to do that as well."

She smiled just faintly. "Thank you... even if I don't remember it."

"So... what now? Different points of view and all?"

She took a breath. "Oh well. Okay. Your sister – what does she like?"

"Oh. Umm..." He shrugged. "Dunno."

Evidently, they were not a close family. "How will I know... well... what will be suitable for her?"

"She's not staying long. I figured you would know. Just whatever you like."

She sat down on a pile of the split logs, puzzled. "I don't even know what I like."

"Pretty sure anything you do will be better than what I have... which is nothing."

"Anything?" The furrow in her brow deepened.

He grinned. "Anything... as long as it is plain-weave."

She smiled. That gave her hope, because she could actually do better than that. Years in a textile sweatshop, and then working as a seamstress assistant meant she could make things. "What about curtains?"

"At the windows? Sure…"

"Would you like a floor rug near the bed?" She was encouraged when he looked impressed.

"I have some pelts you could use. The good ones I sell, and I've tanned some. You might be able to use them… or the leather."

"You make leather? What do you use?"

He shrugged. "Whatever I can get… kangaroo, possum, dingo, sheep hides."

"No, no… I meant your tanning solutions. Are they expensive?"

"Prices in the scrub are mainly in time and effort. Wattle is the best. There's a lot on the ridge that runs up into the Gilyard Ranges… over the back."

She tilted her head with a rather amazing realisation. "You can just go and get things like that whenever you want?"

"Sure. Like I said… time and effort."

"Then you are rich." His wealth may not look like a big stone mansion with drapes and floor carpets, but he could access whatever he needed.

"Huh." He savoured that idea. No one had alluded to him being rich; at least, not in a long time. "Maybe you are right." And he tackled the next log with renewed vigour.

She watched the energy in his stroke as he was hewing the log, dressing it with his broad axe. For someone who never seemed to be in a hurry, Zachary Logan certainly got through plenty of work.

5.

Tibby 'aahhhed' with delight as she undid the bundle of sewing things that had been parcelled up. Zach smiled and was pleased the shop assistant had convinced him to buy this collection. But the hardest thing was cutting that first bolt of fabric. She measured lengths for curtains and then, every afternoon, sat with her feet up and sewed. Zach brought in some sapling poles and secured them over the window frames as curtain rods. She started on other things that might be needed. She measured tea-towels and bath linen. She kept every off-cut and scrap. She braided padded strips together for a floor mat and then backed it with hessian. She made a tote-bag with pockets and sections for keeping her sewing things ordered.

That idea of getting tanning solutions from the scrub around the farm got her thinking. If the bush could yield those solutions, could there also be something that would offer dyes for example? She craved colour. Of course, there wouldn't be anything remotely resembling the rich hues that was used in the finishing mills at home. Here, she rationalised, brown could only logically produce brown... but even shades of brown might break up the sameness. When she asked Zach if he had heard of using bush-dyes to colour fabric, he sort of smiled. It was a vague sort of indulgent grin as if he had never heard of anything so whimsical. He shrugged. "Can't say I have." And that was that.

In the evenings, they sat by the lamplight and Zach listened to her read. They'd work their way through a Bible story. She enjoyed sitting with their mug of tea, chatting about how those people, with all their problems, included God or left Him out.

One morning they were sitting outside on the stumps near the wood heap, having their routine breakfast of tea and damper. Tibby looked at him contentedly munching on his slab of damper with lashings of wild honey. He wanted to make his hut more homely, yet here they were, still balancing plates on their laps. "I have my list here. We don't seem to be making much progress." It was frustrating her no end.

"Well, until the new room's done, I won't be able to get to it."

"Huh." Then something dawned on her. The very first question he asked her was whether or not she could she read. She scanned her memory. He owned a couple of books of poetry and a volume on farming, but he never read them. The occasional newspaper that came from town was for wrapping things, not reading. Not that this bothered her. Her family never had books. That was something she noticed in the manor-houses... bookshelves and reading chairs. She had worried he might think she was not smart. But if he couldn't read, her help was more than sewing. She felt her irritation subside, ebbing away like a tide going out. Her grin broadened. "Okay. I'll put the list away." She went over and threw it on the fire. "Consider it filed," she said with a light laugh.

He felt his shoulders relax. Man, she was pretty when she smiled.

6.

With extra rest each day, Tibby's strength still didn't return. She felt constantly drained and dizzy, like someone had pulled the plug out the end of the wooden dying troughs from home. She'd stop every few paces, hanging on as the hut spun around like rinse water swirling down the drain. Nothing felt right. She struggled to even eat. And when she did the relentless nausea turned her stomach until she vomited.

Zach came in one morning after tending to his animals and sat down with a mug of tea. He looked edgy but didn't say anything. Eventually Tibby put down her sewing. "What is it?"

"Nothing."

"This isn't nothing. You have something to say."

"Well... I do... sort of."

She sighed. It was inevitable. Her poor health was a liability. She had no idea what she would do or where she would go. Yet she told herself most severely that she would not allow herself to be a burden to him. She said nothing but stood up and walked unsteadily over to her bunk. She pulled out her old canvas carry bag and placed it on the bed. She started to slowly fold up her things and pack them away. She swallowed. She would not cry.

"What are you doing?" Zach stared at her confused and then swore as he realised what she was doing. "Tibby! No! I just noticed some things and I'm wondering about 'em. You don't have to go anywhere. Tibby!"

"Oh." She sat down heavily on her bunk. They fell into silence. But regardless of what he said this time, eventually she would have to leave. *"If you don't work, you don't eat"*. The Rector in her neighbourhood would preach this lesson frequently, even when it was a rule that was constantly broken in her family. "Okay..." she said finally, bracing herself she stowed her bag back under the bunk. "Say what you will."

"Well... you are constantly sick, and I was wondering... if you had considered... if it was possible... that you were... well, you know..."

She shook her head vaguely. "Know what?"

"Well... you're pale. And tired. And..."

"I am well aware that I'm not robust," she said resigned. She had no strength to resist anymore. She had always been strong: physically and emotionally. Janie used to say that. *"You're the tough one Tibby. It is never going to be the same when you go."* She was so grateful that her sister could not see her now.

"I hear you well enough," said Tibby. She had been cramping yesterday and it was worse today. "I really should be strong enough to help around a bit." Another wave of nausea hit her as she stood to her feet.

"Tibby. Sit down. You are not hearing me." He reached out and pushed her gently back onto the bunk. "I was wondering more about *why* it is taking so long. Have you considered whether you... well, could you be...?" He shrugged and looked significantly at her abdomen. She had been here over two months. There had been no menstrual evidence.

"What? Oh!" She gasped as his meaning dawned on her. "You think I am up-the-duff? No... No... you are wrong. I started yesterday. I am fine."

"You're bleeding?" He looked concerned.

"Zach these are not things I would ever talk to a man about." She laughed shrilly, and it sounded weird.

"Who else are you going to talk to about it?" He stared at her face. It drained of all colour. Her lip quivered as the cramping started again.

"Zach, thank you for your concern, but I am a woman. These things are perfectly normal. Soon I will be able to do things to help repay your kindness." She stood up to make her point and walked over to the water pail to ladle out a drink. She wavered like an apparition and collapsed on the floor before he could reach her. Blood oozed from under her skirt.

Zach lifted her onto the bunk and then left. He returned later with Old Hilda on his horse, carrying a pack on his shoulder as he walked beside her. There were another couple of bags strapped to the saddle.

Old Hilda was best described as stout woman. There was a roundness to her leathery face and her lips wove around her missing teeth in a rather uneven gummy line. She probably was not as old as her designation suggested, but her skin bore the marks of hardship. Her clothes were dull from grime, and she didn't smile. She stood at the end of the bed and looked at its contents, like one might consider a jar of pickles, to see if they were worth her bother to open the lid.

Tibby's face was porcelain white; her lips had faded to grey. For a second Zach wondered if she hadn't made it. But then she groaned and tried to roll over. Zach didn't feel impatient very often, but now urgency was burning holes in his head. The wads of fabric he had wedged between her legs were soaked with clots. He glanced at Hilda. "Can't you help?"

She shrugged. She went to her bag and unrolled its contents. It contained a rudimentary selection of potions, and odd instruments – some of them obviously homemade. She slowly looked at a couple of things as if she was undecided. "Boil the billy," was all she said.

That gave Zach focus. He brought in one steaming billy and a bowl of water. He put another on the fire. When it boiled, he brought that in too. She made an infusion using some unlabelled powder and stood it to the side to cool. She gave instructions on what was to be taken and for how long. Zach hovered around, ripping up some fabric from the bolts he'd brought from town. He folded them ready in case they were needed. Hilda quietly stepped back from the bed and waited. "What are you doing?" he asked confused.

"Nothin'," she said.

"I know it's pretty bad, but surely you can do something?"

"Can't do it with you here. This is biyani – women's business." Her mouth pressed into that fleshy uneven line again. "Could've stayed home," she said unimpressed. She turned and started to pack up her things.

"Hilda, I came to you because I heard you know things. Please!"

"Nothing personal, but you need to go. Dig something, build something, chop something. Don't care what. Just not here."

He looked outside and saw the dark silhouettes of some women with dilly-bags standing against the shadows of the trees behind the house. They said nothing. He glanced at her. "Woman's business?"

She shrugged again. "They won't come while you're here. Biyani. They know many things, but we got to do it their way..." Hilda started humming an unusual rhythm that sounded odd to his European ears.

Zach grabbed his hat, stoked the fire, and put on another billy of water. He quickly hitched up Bob and took the water cart down to the lagoon. He nursed Tibby back from the brink of death, but now suddenly it was women's business, and he couldn't be involved? In a moment of revelation, he realised that it was because she was a woman, and he was a man, that he was involved. He took his crowbar and shovel out to a paddock not far from the house. He spent the day grubbing out tree stumps in a paddock in an agitated frenzy. As the sun started to dip, he went down to the lagoon and washed up.

There was a stillness about the house as he approached. Old Hilda and her friends were gone, and so were their swags and bags. Tibby was sleeping and there was a wrapped pudding of soiled linen and clothes by door. He went over to her bunk and hunkered down beside her, she rolled over and looked at him and smiled faintly through a euphoric haze. "I think Ol' Hilda is right... I have a good man here," and then she closed her eyes and dozed again.

Zach sat frozen for a long time. That notion... how she said it... it made his chest ache. Him and Tibby... oh yes, he was involved – very involved.

7.

Diligently, Tibby drank Hilda's tea concoction... and nibbled on the roots the women had left. The bleeding continued... but was getting lighter. She forced herself to eat. Forced herself to move. Forced herself to work. She even forced herself to sew. And the more she stitched, the less it seemed like a chore. It became a way to channel the pain, and the unthinkable idea that hate and agony had conceived life. What was equally unimaginable was the sadness she felt now that life was over. She never expected that; she did not expect her grief.

She also hadn't expected that her sewing would become a way of creating something out of the emptiness she felt. She wrote out lists for herself... and felt no need to apologise for them. Zach would bring her things from town... ribbons, buttons, coloured thread and even a pair of fancy scissors. There was also the gift of a notebook for writing. She didn't write down practical stuff, but private explorations of the inner things of her soul. She knew it was safe. It was gratifying to know that it didn't matter what she wrote or where she left it... since Zach couldn't read.

One day when Zach returned from town, he had something wrapped in a bundle of hessian on the cart. He carried it inside and sat it in the middle of the room. She stared at him confused as he stood there with a mysterious grin on his face. "I bought something."

"What is it?"

"Well, it's... just unwrap it."

"For me?" She pulled aside the yards of hessian that was wound around and around. Then there was some sheeting, and she pulled that off as well. It revealed... a sewing machine. She stared at it bewildered.

"You don't like it? Even if you've never used one, I thought that..." His voice faded. Now he was confused.

"Don't you like the way I sew?"

"Well of course I do. That is the point."

"It is? How?"

"Well. There are so many things you want to do. I thought this could help you with the routine sewing so you can spend more time on the more interesting parts... like that fancy stitching that you do. You can't do that with a machine." He pulled over a stool and encouraged her to sit at it. She sat there awkwardly... and eventually reached out and touched it tentatively. Within the week she had worked out how to thread it, adjust the tension, and soon the treadle was whirring away at a great rate.

Days stretched into weeks. Weeks into another month... and another. Project after project were being crossed off her list. Zach made a hutch with shelves, and chairs for the dining table. She made chair cushions, filling them with old rags and scraps of material that she teased and frayed. She filled the linen press with a set of sheets for her bunk and Zach's swag, pillowcases, bath linen and even a tablecloth. She started sewing clothes... a shirt for Zach; an apron and skirt for herself. She made a pinafore for Hilda and sent Zach to deliver it.

Zach started working on the double bed for the new room. Tibby made up the mattress ticking for the bed, and a round of double bed linen as well. Zach bought a bale of sheep's wool from the neighbours to stuff the mattress. They made new pillows with feathers salvaged from the chook yard, and the occasional cockerel they baked. Zach ordered some sought-after geese from the market in town, but it was uncertain when they would be available.

Working on the bedroom bombarded Tibby's mind with questions she didn't have the courage to voice. Was Zach planning to be married? Did he visit a girl when he went to town? Was his sister bringing a new husband with her? The questions were just wordlessly there; just as Zach was just there. Two people silently working side by side.

This was a comfortable working liaison, a soothing balm of routine. This life was so different from her volatile childhood. Little Tibby would run from their little tenement stone building and hide in the cold, and the wet, behind a disused coal cart with the neighbour's dog, until the crashing faded in the early morning hours.

But eventually the sameness of the Dellaweir routine melted into a monotony that began to gnaw at her. Even the bland colour of the plain-weave seemed to reinforce the tedium. And Zach always bought more home when he went into town for supplies.

Late one afternoon, Zach came in and put his upturned hat on the table. "This is for you." She stared at the black, sweat soaked leather band around the brim of his hat and sort of cringed. "Not the hat. You don't get that. What's inside..."

"Oh." She looked curiously at the abundance of curly rust-coloured pods that he had piled inside.

"I thought about what you said. I wondered if these might work... you know, about what you were saying..."

Tabitha looked bewildered. She had no idea what he was referring to.

"For your sewing stuff... the curtains and cushions and covers and such. You said you wanted to try dying colour into them. I asked around some. No one was really sure, but Ol' Hilda thought the bush women boiled these pods to give colour for their weaving. I've been waiting for them to ripen, so you could try and see what comes out."

Tibby's jaw dropped. He hadn't dismissed or forgotten her query at all... but it was percolating away, waiting until he had something to offer. She sprang up and gave him an enormous hug. "Thank you! This is perfect!"

He nodded and swallowed awkwardly, and the went to stoke the fire for dinner.

This collection started her on a project of scientific proportions. She pulled out the pods and boiled them. The seeds had an unusual tone of dark rust, so she boiled them separately. She cut squares of fabric so that she could see what colour might take, and what might not. She tried some with vinegar; some with salt. Some she boiled in his aluminium pot and some in his iron pot; some she soaked cold. She talked to Zach about her ideas of sampling other things as sources of dye colour. Zach joined her in becoming a forager of all sorts of potential dye-items: bark, roots, leaves. Almost anything became a prospective dye-pot. Her discoveries of different shades, and washability of the results intrigued her, and she enthusiastically described her results over dinner and wrote them in her notebook. She was fascinated by the difference between what she expected and what actually happened. The beautiful red beets Zach brought in from the town market-garden stained her fingers crimson and the fabric a dull sort of dark beige. And then the beige onionskins gave her an intriguing deep yellow. When the wattle was flowering, he gathered a big bunch, and it became an exciting experiment in gold. She loved that colour so much she pulled down the curtains and subjected them to a golden bath. The cushion covers also took a dunking. She laughed and cried and sweated over those pots.

One evening, Zach sat in the squatter's chair while Tibby was working by the dim glow of the lamp on the table. She was impatient to see how her samples of dyed squares could be patch-worked together as a quilt for the bed. She placed block after block, rotating and swapping the colours to create a pattern in the fabrics and then she pinned them to a backing sheet to hold their position while she mapped the design. It was coming together beautifully.

He cleared his throat. "Tibby..."

"Hu-hum..." She swapped over a couple squares and tilted her head in focused concentration as she considered how they looked together.

"Tibby..."

"Yeah..." She changed another couple of squares and pinned them.

"Tibby... I want you to marry me."

"Hmmm?"

"Tibby... will you marry me."

"Oh!" She jabbed her finger with a pin and sucked in the pain. When she looked up, he was staring at her.

"Will you marry me?" he repeated. She stared back at him. "Aren't you going to say anything?"

"Umm. I don't know what to say. I didn't know you wanted me to stay."

"I want you to stay. I don't want you to go... And I'm damn sure I don't want you going over to Bates' place. That ain't right."

"Oh." Her mind was spinning. So, although he didn't particularly want to marry her, he was prepared to do so, to save her from an unfortunate alliance. "I thought I was just helping you out some."

"You are helping me. More than just sewing. More than you know."

"Oh."

"I know this isn't the most genteel courting ever done. But when I bring you flowers, you just end up stewing them." He sat in the shadows watching the play of emotion on her face.

Tibby looked at him sitting there and she became aware that she had been holding her breath for an indeterminate time, waiting for knell that would signal she would have to go. Suddenly she could breathe again. She started to cry.

Zach jumped to his feet and was beside her in a moment. "Hush now. I didn't mean to upset you none. You don't have to. I won't be making you. Hush now..." And she grabbed him and clung to him, some loose squares spilling to the floor. As she wedged against his hard chest, she realised she never wanted to let him go. Slowly it dawned on him that her tears were 'yes'. And he kissed the crown of her head and she thought that her heart would explode from happiness as he slid a very simple ring on her finger.

Tibby woke in a sweat. Her was neck stiff from where she rested on her arms at the table. More squares had fallen from her lap where she was sitting on the chair. She looked over at the empty squatter's chair, and could hear Zach's quiet breathing, regular in sleep, from his swag where he had moved it into the new bedroom. The bedframe was pushed up against the wall. He didn't seem to be in a hurry to finish the mattress. The lamp had burnt out and she traced the empty finger on her left hand. The moon shone through the shutters and the realisation washed over her that it had been a dream. A beautiful dream. It had felt so real. Tabitha came to Australia to marry... pure and simple, but she was also driven by a niggling idea that there must be more. 'More' than the way it was at home.

Her mother used frying-skillets to make a point. The mistress-seamstress insisted on screaming. She grew up with people who believed effective communication depended on its volume. She had hoped that in coming here she would experience a different *approach* to doing life, not just a different location.

Zach's quiet way was different in every way to what she was used to. She remembered how, once or twice, she had seen a particular couple from the textile mills. Young they were, and in love, and they didn't fight. They spoke to each other with such earnestness that her ears burned to know of the intimate things they spoke of. She had forgotten how taken she was by the idealism of that picture, as they walked past the waterwheels that lifted the murky waters out of the channels for the factories. What would it be like step into that picture with Zach? Was it possible that this dream might be fulfilled in the little hut on Dellaweir Station?

She wiped the beads of perspiration from her forehead and went to the pail and dipped herself a pannikin of water. She glanced through the doorway of the room where Zach lay, bare chested, in his swag. She hardly knew where to look. Not like she hadn't seen his skin before, but just now, every knot, every ripple, every muscle seemed so desirable. She stared at him for a long time, embarrassed by her mesmerised fascination. Would a man this cautious ever hold her in his arms like the dream that had disturbed her naivety? Would he ever talk to her in those quiet whispered tones of that water-wheel couple? He slept on, unaware of the realisation that filled her senses from the lingering sweetness of that kiss from her dreams.

She shook herself and lay down on her bed and stared at the shadows on the ceiling of the hut. What would she do now? After all, he was working on improving this house for his sister, not for her, not them. She closed her eyes and willed herself to sleep. But her mind refused to quieten. She had never been aware of him like this, and it frightened her. What if he sensed what she felt? Would he throw her out if she gave the slightest hint? He had said, right at the beginning: board and lodging, until she could travel. Could she invent more projects to legitimise her staying? Something had changed, and he had done nothing to change it. It was just a dream, and yet it changed everything. And she rolled over and cried. She had lost something incredibly safe and comforting and lovely. Before this, all she was ever doing was more sewing. She wished she could go back and stay unaware and comfortable. In a way she wished she could un-dream the dream. Now she was in territory that was unknown and uncomfortable and frightening and tantalising and exciting... and she could not go back.

In her dream, the man asked the girl and the girl said yes: that was the proper way of things. But this was Zach. What if he was so staid and so content, that he would never ask? Was it possible to die an old maid, living with a man she loved?

Oh.

And yet, surely as she breathed, being here was so much better than being somewhere else. Anywhere else. She pulled up the heavy felt blanket in the cool hours of the morning and resolved within herself that she would do whatever she needed to stay. He had to see that she was no longer the invalid, but she was well and useful. Not just in the role of a willing seamstress but in all sorts of matters. But she was not going to seduce him, or cajole him, or bully him into formalising anything. If this was going to happen, he had to be the one to initiate it. Yes, she would out-wait Zachary Logan... until she was ninety if needs be.

8.

"Morning." She opened her eyes to see him standing over her bunk with a mug of tea. "You must have been sewing to all hours... the lamp burnt out."

Instinctively she pulled her nightgown around her, as she saw him standing there in his sleeveless vest, the image of him in the night shadows still imprinted on her mind. She blushed and sat up. She reached out to take the mug, and her hand touched his. She jolted, knocking his hand and the tea slopped onto the floor.

"Oh, my goodness. I'm so sorry. Still asleep..." She covered her eyes, embarrassed by the blush that ran up her neck.

"Did it burn you?" Would she always be so edgy around him? He worked so patiently to be reassuring. Safe. He wanted her to feel protected.

"No. No. I'm okay. Thank you." She grabbed her shawl and swung her legs out over the bed and walked over to the table and sat down. She pushed aside the fabric montage that was still laid out on the table and blushed again at the memory of her dream and rubbed her empty ring-finger. This was not going to be easy. She drank deeply and regulated her breathing. She could do this. "I was thinking. I've have not really seen much of Dellaweir beyond the hut here. I was wondering if I could go with you... and have a look around."

He looked at her then, curious at the pang of concern that nailed him in the chest. He wasn't ready for her to be trying her out wings. Not yet. "You're feeling up to that?"

"Yeah. I think so. A change of scenery might inspire my projects. Sometimes it feels a bit stale. I think some fresh air might help."

"Oh. Okay. Well, I'm going down to the billabong first thing..." That felt harmless enough. Suddenly he had this need to keep her close. Very close.

He hitched Bob in his billygoat harness and led him, pulling the water-cart, down to the billabong to fill up the barrel for household use. Tibby stood on the tailgate and swayed with the gentle rhythm of Bob's tread. She looked up through the gums, their elongated branches stamping patterns against the rich blue of the sky. She smiled. This was her first billy-cart ride, ever. If only Janie could see her now.

Zach had constructed a crude platform out over the large water hole that he referred to as The Billabong. It was fed by the creek from the mountains, creating a natural weir that levied along the contours of the creek banks before it fed downstream into the river that flowed through the valley. This permanent lagoon was Dellaweir's richest asset. Zach never underestimated it.

Bob was tethered on the platform and waited patiently while Zach started to bail water into the barrel in a synchronised, choreographed rhythm. He swung around, filling the barrel in one movement using a billycan on a pole while standing on the platform. Tibby watched this mundane, routine chore with fascination. Zach had done life solo very capably for years. How was it even possible she could ever be useful to him?

He glanced up and saw the intensity of her watching and something almost like pride swelled in his chest. "Never had an audience doing this before. Feels odd." Nice though.

She blushed and turned away. She didn't want him to feel uncomfortable. That would be terrible. She wanted him... to... well... be easy with her in her life. Yes, that is what she was aiming for. She stepped forward. "Is there anything I can do to help?"

"Well... I've sort of rigged it up to be a one-man job."

"Oh." She stepped back.

He quickly gathered his thoughts. "Nearly done. Only got to fill up the water bags now." He took off his shirt and stepped down into the water hole. He swam out from the platform and then came back, and he stood up shaking his wet hair out of his eyes like a shaggy dog. "Can you pass me the bags then... one at a time?"

"Sure." She nodded and picked one of the canvas bags off the hook where it was hanging. She stepped around the cart and dropped it into his open hands. He looked up at her and grinned. She blushed again, turning away. She wanted to jump into his arms. Foolishness.

"Hey?"

"Yes?" She turned back almost eager.

"There's two more." And he handed up the dripping bag.

"Oh." She was flustered and she quickly reached down. The weight of the bag took her by surprise, and she toppled, landing on him with a scream. She flayed and splashed and spluttered. He grabbed her and held her steady. Her breath was rasping, her heart beating wildly, and she squeezed her eyes shut. Mortifying. He was so close... and she held her breath.

She felt him brush the wet hair out of her eyes and she looked at him, his eyes laughing. "Keen. I was going to hand it up to you." He didn't seem irritated.

"Oh you!" And she splashed him playfully. "I wanted to help."

"Ah-huh."

She shrugged. She had no response. Tongue tied.

"All in a day's work... collecting water; saving you from drowning."

She scoffed. "Drowning? I can stand up."

"You aren't doing much standing," he said with a wry twist on his lips. She was still clinging to him. "And we now have lost the water-bag."

She quickly found her footing and stepped back as he felt around with his toe and then duck dived and emerged holding up the missing bag. "Saved. One damsel and one water-bag."

"No doubt I should be grateful..."

"Oh, you are grateful. I can tell."

He hoisted himself onto the platform, and patted Bob, patiently bemused by the disturbance. Zach threw down the remaining two bags, hitting the water with a slap. He sat on the edge, his ankles dangling in the water as she stood in the water bedraggled, while she unscrewed the caps and filled them, handing them up to him.

"So how did you know?"

She shrugged. "Know what?"

"That having a swim is best part of this particular chore?"

"Really? You think I did this on purpose?"

"I do it on purpose."

"But I can't swim."

"You should consider learning. Makes water-carrying the best chore in the day."

He reached down, and she took his wrist. He pulled her small dripping frame up beside him. They sat for a while, dangling their ankles in swirls of water before walking back to the house and while he unhitched the cart, she went inside and changed her wet clothes, and then returned to her sewing.

9.

When Zach went to town again, Tibby privately wondered when she might feel brave enough to tackle that trip. Not yet. She'd take the opportunity to focus on piecing her quilt undisturbed.

When he arrived home, and attended to the chores outside, he came in and sat down at the table to eat the meal Tibby had ready for him. He drank his tea, and then dug into his pocket. "Got a letter today. Think it's from Heather. Wondered if you'd care to read it?" He handed her the unopened envelope.

"Your sister! She's coming?"

"Dunno. This is the first letter I've had from her."

She opened it and read it out loud. Zach coughed and quickly guzzled the last of his tea, blinking his eyes. Tibby looked at him confused. "Are you okay? You seem... pale." The correspondence was brief and gave the details of her travel arrangements. She would arrive the following fortnight on the coach.

"Oh. I guess. Just lots to do." He swallowed and shook his head. Bewildered.

Yes, suddenly there were many things to finalise. Tibby wrote out another list, planning every minute so that the guest room would be ready for this honoured member of the family. The bale of wool for the mattress-filling was teased and packed into the casing. She used leather buttons to pull it in and hold the bulbous pillow in place.

Tibby was disappointed that there was no way she could finish quilting the project in time, but she backed it and consoled herself that at least there was a rather lovely patch-worked throw to cover the plain felt blankets.

54

The floor was scrubbed, and the linen washed again. She even tackled the outdoor kitchen area making it a little less like a campsite and hoped that it might offer some rustic appeal in its basic setup. She used some of her dyed samples as doilies and brought in bush flowers to stand on the dresser.

At the end of that frantic fortnight, they stood and looked around at the house prepared for their guest. Zach reached out and touched her shoulder awkwardly. "Thanks..."

"That was quite a task you set yourself. Even though... well... it doesn't seem like this is something you've been looking forward to. Do you get along with your sister?"

"We haven't spoken for years..." But he didn't elaborate, and spoke of more practical things, like storing his swag under her bunk during the day so that the guest room would be available for Heather's exclusive use.

Zach put on a clean shirt and hitched the horse up to his small cart and went into town to meet the coach and his visitor. Tibby tidied last minute things and set about cooking a special dinner. She felt nervous, not so much for herself, but for Zach and this long-awaited stay-over. It seemed that he considered he was being bestowed a visit of great condescension and generosity by his sister coming at all.

Even if that was the impression Tibby had acquired, nothing prepared her for the way Heather swept into the room, grunting about the discomfort of the trip, and frowning at the frugal simplicity of the hut. Zach followed her inside carrying a heavy trunk, which he placed under the window with a thud. There were a number of cumbersome luggage cases that he took to her room.

"Really, Zachary, you knew I was coming. I did think you would make an effort. Especially as I was accompanied by my good friend Amelia..." She caught sight of Tibby and paused midsentence. "Oh. Who are you?"

Tibby glanced towards Zach who averted his eyes. Tibby curtsied and nodded. "Tabitha, Ma'am."

Heather stared at her for a moment and then quickly diverted her attention to Zach. "Really, Zachary... who is this woman?" Then in horror she accused, "I do hope you are not married? How embarrassing! Or perhaps you are not! That would be even more horrifying! You always insist on resisting every moral convention. Why is she even here?"

Zach's eyes held contempt. "We are not married. And if we were, it is not my problem that you might be embarrassed."

Tibby saw that look. Zach was a patient man, but she recognised instantly that every fibre in his body was being stretched. Every ounce of anticipation evaporated; every needle prick she had endured patiently seemed such a waste. Then there was a rattle on the verandah, and another lady appeared at the door struggling with a stack of hatboxes.

Heather turned around, and said to the doorway, "Well goodness, don't just stand there: help her." Tabitha quickly relieved her of some of her burden, ushering her into the next room. Zach stood, planted, unmoved by their predicament. Heather went over to him and whispered something quite severely. He turned away and gave his attention to chopping wood.

The hatbox lady emerged from their room. Heather rushed to comfort her like a child with a scraped knee. "Amelia darling, I am so sorry. This really is something! I had no idea the circumstances would be so paltry. I'm sure these conditions in time will be improved."

Tibby nearly laughed out loud; and then went to check the special dinner that now seemed like scraps.

Zach stopped chopping when he saw her leaning over the fire. He wanted to say something, but just now his irritation was beyond words. He leant his axe against the splitting stump and came over, standing by the lean-to. "I brought another barrel from town today. Would you come to help me fill up the water cart tomorrow? In the morning..."

Perhaps these foreigners would not change their routine much after all. She was sure they had arrived from some far exotic land with strange costumes and bizarre customs. She smiled softly at his frown. "Only if I can have a swim."

His shoulders seemed to relax just the slightest bit. "The best part."

Amelia unpacked a case of painted china, washed off the packing sawdust and set the table with great care. Dinner was a torturous exercise, and Zach struggled to stay civil. He grunted with uncharacteristic frankness while Heather trumpeted about her trip, her charities, her friend, and her poor blessed departed husband – Mr Harold Granger, God-rest-his-soul... and his persecuted saintly mother, Mrs Granger. She had been one of Aunt Peony's most faithful companions. The table setting had been one of Aunt Peony's. Not her best one of course, but a very fine every-day setting. Heather was pleased she had such foresight to bring it along and she bemoaned a chip in one of the cups. Amelia sat, looking coyly at Zachary, with a giggly smile on her lips.

Tibby hardly knew where to direct her attention. If she looked at Heather, she was greeted with a scowl and a barrage of accusations as if she was completely responsible for the treachery Heather had to endure to get there. If she looked at Amelia, it seemed to invite a smothering of vague and mind-numbing comments, which was the last thing she intended to subject herself to. If she looked at Zach, she almost had to hold herself between crying and laughing, neither of which would have been considered appropriate in the present company.

At one point, Heather made a particularly obnoxious comment about the inadequacy of their situation, and Tibby instinctively reached out under the table and held Zach's clenched fist. He quickly looked at her beside him and she held his hand quietly, avoiding his gaze. He stared at his plate, his scrutiny of the bits of stewed carrots challenging her expectation of restraint. She said nothing, and after a while his hand relaxed, and he went back to eating his meal.

Heather glared directly at Tibby. "Where are you sleeping tonight?" she demanded.

Tibby blinked. "Where I always do, I guess."

"Oh, my dear, I know you can't possibly mean that little stretcher in the corner because Amelia will need that bunk tonight."

Zach put down his knife. "Your guest will have to share the double bed." Tibby noted that he was very definite that she was not his guest.

"Share?" Heather choked, "I'm not going to share a bed!"

"Well, I can make up a swag, and you can fight over that if you prefer."

"But that is ridiculous. There is a perfectly suitable bunk over there."

"Yes. And Tabitha will be using it."

"Well, that is incredibly ill-mannered of you, Zachary! Common hospitality demands that visitors get to sleep in *beds*. You are still very much the rude little boy I grew up with. Some things never change."

"So, it would seem. We're not big on etiquette here. Tibby is staying in her own crib."

Heather huffed and puffed, but on this Zach would not be moved. Afterwards, as they washed up the dishes on the planks outside, Tibby gently said, "Zach, if it's easier, I'm happy to use a swag while they are here..."

"Yes, of course you are. This is not about your willingness. It is about their presumption and dismissal of your needs. You are staying in your bunk. They will have to share. That bed is perfectly adequate."

"Are you sure?" She expected him to be relieved and relent. His defence of her comfort was gratifying. He had not even mentioned that he had given up the bunk for her and used a swag himself since she arrived.

"I am sure." And he held up his hand as she went to object. The subject was closed.

In the early morning they walked down to the creek leading the goat and cart. Zach needed space. He hardly even noticed that he expected that space to be shared with Tibby.

He tethered Bob, but he didn't go straight to work. Instead, he sat down on the platform and with a slight gesture invited Tibby to sit beside him. They looked over the still water; the mist rising off the surface of the lagoon; the occasional ripple dispersed as a fish skimmed to the surface. The dawn sky broke through the trees and shimmered across the breeze-dimpled water like diamonds being scattered. They said nothing for a long time.

"I have a million questions," she said eventually.

"I bet you do..." He turned towards her as the sunlight spilled over her hair like golden shawl. He looked into her eyes. It was not a breathless, kiss-me sort of gaze, but something quieter and deeply connected. "No questions today. But don't worry, I will have to cart water for the house every morning now... extra company means we use more water. There will be plenty of time for talking." Zach did his daily chores with religious diligence, but he never rushed. This was something he wasn't going to rush either.

Time. That reassured her. Perhaps it was a realisation that she had witnessed Zach work very hard. He had completed the room extension, all from scratch. He had chopped, and dressed, and hewn every plank, and split every roofing shingle. He'd built furniture, and sure, they weren't fine classical pieces, with ornate inlays... but it was solid and functional. Tibby decided she didn't consider his work clever, but it was never half-hearted, and it was certainly not shabby.

After they filled the barrel and water bags, he paused. "Still want that swim?"

Tibby almost choked. "Oh goodness, I was kidding. Can we do that?"

"Given I own the place... pretty sure we have permission."

"But what would your sister say?"

"About what?"

"About swimming... in a lagoon... together..."

"She's not big on sports. Don't think she'll understand."

"I was thinking about whether she would consider it proper."

His eyes turned a little cold. "You're very astute, Tibby Flanders. Heather is *very* big on proper. What would you do if she was not here to give her pompous opinion?"

The morning was already warming up. She boldly took off her pinafore and boots. "I'd fall in, I guess." And she jumped off the pier like an eight-year-old. She gasped at the coolness of the water and spluttered to the surface. One balmy summer day she remembered splashing in the canals at home with her brothers. It was the only time she could remember pretending her life was just like a holiday at the beachside.

Zach was there when she surfaced. "Can you float?" he asked with a smirk as she floundered to find her footing.

She raised her brow incredulously. "Float?"

He helped her test the weightlessness of the water, the coolness of it washing over her limbs, the fabric of her garments clinging to her body. His hand supported the arch of her back as she looked up past the trees and their leaves, past the sky and the clouds drifting past in the morning light. It seemed like time was suspended in the weightlessness of the water and she surrendered to the buoyancy of the moment. Perhaps life was not like a holiday at the beach... but some moments were.

That evening after dinner, as they sat around the lamp, Zach put the bible on the table. Tibby was a bit surprised that he was going to insist on their usual routine, and every so often she glanced up at him as she read. He sat there, quietly ignoring Heather's restless huffing in the shadowed recesses of the room. Amelia came over and sat mutely until Zach asked her, "What did you think about the story?"

"Oh! Well! I think it is a very interesting story..."

"Which part in particular?" he insisted.

"Well, I think Joseph sounds like he would make a good husband," she said innocently.

Tibby looked down at the table, embarrassed. This was awkward. Zach didn't seem fazed, maybe even amused. "What makes him husband material do you think?"

"Well... umm... I'm not sure. He is handsome and clever. He managed the whole estate. And... he is a good person! I wouldn't want a husband who was running after all sorts of types. That happened to my Aunt Agnes, and it broke her heart. The kids growing up all wild now. Uncle Benny wasn't a good husband type at all."

"It is an important decision for sure."

Heather stood up and cleared her throat with the very distinct message she was summoning Amelia to assist her in retiring. Amelia blushed and giggled, and then fled to the bedroom with Heather.

Tibby couldn't help herself. "She thinks you are her Joseph you know."

He grinned. "Handsome and clever? It's nice to know someone thinks so."

"You know it isn't fair... leading her on like that when you aren't serious." Breaking her heart ... my heart.

"I'd never lead someone on, unless my intentions were honourable." He looked into Tibby's eyes and willed her to see his intention was to be as honest and as straight as any Joseph. *I'm not leading you on*, he silently declared. *I couldn't be more serious about anything.*

Tibby stared at him for a moment and felt her own heart sinking. She had never considered the possibility that this would be anything other than what she had hoped for. Had she been helping to prepare the house, not for his sister, but for a bride she had brought for him? Was that the plan? Although Zach had always been up-front, she felt duped: the gullible innocent. He never alluded to their relationship being more than a board and lodging arrangement; a business transaction to provide assistance in a task he needed done. She was more like Amelia than she cared to admit. Her presumption was rather embarrassing. Suddenly she didn't have all the time in the world. No, not at all.

Zach waited for her to say something. But Tibby stood up abruptly. "I'm going to bed." She went behind the screen and changed into her nightdress, and quickly slipped under the covers and feigned sleep; her mind rushing with the possibility of being passed over for a naïve, pretty blonde, who was the personal attendant to his sister.

Zach stood for a moment before retrieving his swag from under her bed and looked at her brown hair tumbling over the pillow. He wondered what he was doing wrong here. One moment life was gentle and intimate, sharing the arrival of the morning dawn sitting on a rough bush pier; floating in the water weightlessly; the next moment it was like he was still nursing an injured rabbit kit trembling whenever he came near. His main stay had always been 'don't rush'. But now he felt off balance. Uncertain. Everything he had been working towards over last eight years was about becoming certain... and he thought he was... until this moment. Now he had the very distinct sense something was about to fall through his fingers like river sand if he didn't move decisively.

"Hey? Coming down to the waterhole this morning?" Tibby opened her eyes and tried to focus. "You said you had questions," he prompted in a whisper. She stretched and sat up. Would he really want her to go with him? The lure of getting some answers meant she quickly pulled on her boots while he hitched up the billycart.

They walked down the track together, leading Bob by the halter. Somehow all the fears of last night faded in the streaks of the morning dawn washed clean from an overnight shower. Zach pointed out droplets suspended from grey-green eucalypt leaves in sparkling chandeliers. Tibby found a perfectly spun dreamcatcher of a spider's web, spangled in mist. They took turns in noticing obscure beauties that are the exclusive privilege of early-morning risers. A wallaby joey scrambled for the security of its mother's pouch, and then they bounded away. The enthusiastic morning warble of a magpie broke the silence. They sat on the platform and quietly watched the morning colours fade. Every so often one of them silently pointed: a fish jumping; a kingfisher dive-bombing; a freshwater turtle surfacing.

Eventually Zach looked at Tibby and said, "What is the main question you have?"

She didn't hesitate. "That's simple! How can Heather possibly be your sister?"

"Same mother, same father..." He grinned at the obvious.

"No seriously! You couldn't be more different."

"My mother died when I was four. Father was in the merchant navy. That took him overseas for long periods, so we were sent separate ways. My Uncle Cedric was a very practical man, with little time for book-learning. He thought scholars had their heads in the clouds. That suited me. I wasn't an admirer of school and I wanted to learn farming. My Aunt Peony is like the rest of my mother's family... social climbers with a nose for proper connections. Heather was always a bit of a snob but being with Peony nailed it permanently into her soul. We spent Christmas together every year. They were torturous affairs endured under protest by both of us. We were never close."

Tibby took a moment to absorb it. "So why did she come?"

"I don't really know. Perhaps curiosity got the better of her." He had a fair idea it was more than that.

"Do you know how long she is staying?"

"Nope. Never talked about it. But Heather's very good at telling. She'll tell me when she's ready to go."

"Don't you want it to be different?"

"Me and her? What I want, and what is realistic, are two different things. I realised a long time ago that probably, the only family trait we have common, is that we both are stubborn. Heather's desire to convert me to her social set has been her undaunted mission in life. Besides, Heather is not going to change her spots no matter how much I kick and scream. So now I just let her be. It's one of the reasons I came here. To become comfortable with my own spots."

"Are you comfortable yet?"

"Hmm. I am. I'm very happy with what I've found. And I'm okay that other people, Heather in particular, may not be admirers of my choices."

"Isn't it lonely?"

"It hasn't been... until recently."

"Recently? Something interrupted you?" She said it before she even realised.

"Someone. Yes."

Tibby blinked. If she was the reason for that interrupted calm, he would probably resent her being here. She started to sway unsteadily. He reached out and steadied her and she jolted under his touch.

"But it's been a good discovery, Tibby. I could never miss what I didn't know was possible. I know now what was missing."

Tibby looked out across the water. She wanted to believe she was the reason that was more was unveiled. But he didn't say that. He had every opportunity to say it... and he didn't. She stood to her feet and handed him the pitcher pole. She certainly wasn't going to sit there and listen to him declare his heart for Amelia.

Zach looked up at her hurrying on with the day. He had been so close to telling her outright... but he sensed her discomfort and he hesitated. And now he was grateful. Her avoidance told him she not ready to hear the obvious truth. In this he decided he could wait. It was too important to stampede in and ruin all possibility of seeing this be a reality in his life. If he was okay with the disapproval of some, he was sure he would never be able to make an easy acceptance of one particular rejection.

Amelia came over to Zach, smiling bashfully. "You were out early this morning? Did you see the sun rise?"

"Nope. Can't say I did." He silently mused that he saw the reflection of the pastel colours of the dawn sky burst on the billabong like a mirror. He saw the morning light shine off Tibby's hair, giving her a sort of ethereal halo for an enchanted suspended moment. He decided this was all too sacred to explain to someone as trite as Amelia. He jolted as he saw the clear, unashamed intent in her eyes. He looked suspiciously at his sister and clearly understood why she was willing to denigrate herself by visiting his underprivileged humpy. He was marked as the target in her plan to make Amelia part of the family. Hmm.

He understood his sister's weakness, but he knew nothing of Amelia. In fact, she was the least interesting person he could ever remember crossing paths with. So, he resolved to make her a study.

Amelia leaned into his face and fluttered her eyelashes, which created the bizarre effect that she was having a partial seizure. "I wish I could see the sun rise," she said wistfully.

He looked at her twitching with a sort of schoolboy fascination. He bit his lip and wondered what sort of treatment he would give one of his animals if they were convulsing like this. Then he cheekily proceeded to consider what measures might lessen their suffering. He decided that the most effective way to smother Amelia's domestic ambitions would be a fair dose of realism. "I can't give you a sunrise at nine o'clock in the morning, but I could show you some aspects of farm life. Only Tibby will have to come."

Tibby looked up from her sewing. "Me? Why?"

"Because it would be unseemly to entertain a lady visitor unaccompanied." And privately he added, *'And there is no way I'll let myself be caught alone with this woman'*. She reminded him of a python he found in his chicken coup. It was so bloated from gorging that it was unable to escape. The trapped snake was doomed, but the damage it did to the occupants of that coop was significant.

Tibby's eyes enlarged. "You want me to *chaperone* you?" She felt indignant and tried to focus on her sewing. A lump rose in her throat as she realised that Zach didn't see being with her as unseemly, because, well, he obviously didn't see her as someone he would potentially consider suitable.

Amelia eyes jumped as Tibby said the word 'chaperone', and Zach saw she looked quite victorious. He imagined that there was the clear recitation of wedding chimes making music in her head. He walked over to where Tibby was sewing, and quietly said, "Please do this Tibby. I need you to."

There was such earnestness in his eyes that the speed of her stitching went up a notch. She wondered if he really understood that there was little she could imagine that she would refuse him, if he truly asked it of her. She relented, but the injustice smarted in her throat. It was obvious that Amelia had intentions, but she had not seriously considered that Zach might have Amelia marked as his wife. That he would ask her to chaperone, gave the very clear message that he was more than willing to go along with this happy family charade. It irked her, and not just a little bit, that she had cleaned and scrubbed and cooked and stitched for a simpering woman who was fully intent on snatching Zach right out from underneath her good sewing.

⁂

Zach hitched up the billycart and instructed them to bring along some gloves. He asked Tibby to take Bob's halter while he walked ahead with Amelia. He peppered her with a series of questions; any newspaperman would have been proud of the interview he conducted. "How long have you known my sister?"

She giggled and blushed. "Oh, it doesn't seem like hardly any time at all. But I can't imagine not being with her either. How you must have missed her so."

Zach had his own opinion about that. He framed the same question in a different way. "Hmm. How long have you been my sister's companion?"

"Oh yes, Mrs Granger is such a companionable person. I would love to be her sister too."

"I suppose you could adopt," he said, but when she raised her eyebrows and exclaimed that she didn't know it was possible to adopt adults, he thought he might try a different tact.

"What does your family do?" he asked.

"Oh, my family is not half as interesting as your family..." As a reoccurring expectation, 'interesting' was becoming rather tedious.

"I doubt it." Zach considered his family terminally sick. Generally, he didn't think disease a point of curiosity, rather sympathy. "What about your parents; what do they do?"

"Oh, you know..."

"Nope."

"Well, my mother was an attendant to one of the finer families along the North side and father worked for the shipping companies."

Zach translated: housemaid and docker. He smirked as he acknowledged that his sister's charity to her Charge in marrying-up did not extend to him. Indeed, Heather was right: some things never change.

"My mother introduced me the Grangers. They had a lot to do with Miss Heather's family. So, it was only natural that when Miss Heather married Master Harold that I would be given the opportunity."

"Ahh..." That added a piece to the puzzle.

Tibby heard snippets of their conversation, and frankly thought Zach was being rude. Yet Amelia was blithely unaware. Regardless of how cold, analytical, or sharp Zach made his questions, Amelia giggled and smirked and observed that he was a most interesting person.

Zach stopped where he had chopped down trees to dress timber for the room extension. Some of the stumps had been removed. "Well. Here we are. I am clearing this paddock. Now, we need to pick up the rocks."

"Why?" Amelia looked confused. It didn't seem reasonable to relocate something from its local habitat. Even rocks.

Tibby raised her eyebrows in amusement, yet Zach, with a straight face, respectfully explained, "I'm going to do some stonework in the cottage... well, a cookhouse actually. To do that I need to collect the rocks. Taking them from here, means the pasture will grow better. Tibby is going to lead Bob along, and we'll put the rocks in the cart."

Tibby grabbed Bob's halter and made a move to guide him slowly across the paddock. Zach wasn't annoyed by Amelia's simple questions, rather he seemed to value them. She never thought to ask why. She had no idea he was planning a cookhouse. Here he was, patiently addressing every enquiry Amelia made with the forbearance of beatified saint.

She smarted under that realisation that since her stamina was not robust, Amelia was fast becoming Zach's new best work buddy. She continued to lead Bob by his halter, while they picked rocks, filling the goat-cart. The pace Zach set was unrelenting. It didn't take long to fill the first load. They piled the rocks onto a hard, bare piece of ground, according to size and went back for another load... and another.

Even though leading Bob up and down the paddock was rather undemanding work compared to rock picking, Tibby felt her energy sagging. Finally, Zach look Bob's lead from her hand and said that would do for today. He led the cart back to the house. Amelia helped unload their cargo beside the livestock stables and then Zach tended to the chores, while Tibby went inside and fixed some lunch of damper and salted beef.

She found Heather huffing about being left alone to endure the most tedious of mornings. Heather looked with distain at Amelia's dusty, rubbed gloves, and accosted Zach as he sat down at the table. "Goodness, Zachary, what have you been bothering Amelia with all morning?"

Amelia stepped forward enthusiastically. "Oh no, we had the most interesting morning. We collected rocks of all sizes and put them in piles. We even brought a cartload back so Zach can use them to build a new cookhouse," she said happily.

Zach looked up at the conclusion of this speech; an expression of marvel infusing his eyes. "You enjoyed our outing?" Perhaps there was more than he allowed in dull little Amelia.

"Oh yes! Farm life is very interesting."

Her boredom with the job was forgotten, so he would have to find something else to dampen her enthusiasm for prospective husband material.

Tibby thumped the plate down in front of Zach. "Very interesting," she agreed abruptly; and he raised his brow, smothering a smile as he picked up his fork.

After the evening meal, Tibby could barely keep her eyes open. Instead of bringing the Bible for her to read, Zach stretched exaggeratedly and declared his intention of going to bed early after such a full day. A pout of plaintive disappointment hovered around Amelia's full lips. "Oh, I was so looking forward to some interesting conversation."

Heather rolled her eyes and said to the stratosphere, "Interesting would indeed be a pleasant change."

"Well, I'll leave you to it then," said Zach. "Tibby, can I see you outside for a tick?"

More demands. She followed him outside, exhausted. "Yes, what do you need?"

"Don't worry about Heather and Amelia: between them they can meet their expectations for social conversation." He lifted her hand and held it. "You're asleep on your feet. Go straight to bed. I trust you sleep well."

Gratitude leapt into Tibby's eyes. "Oh, thank you," she said, "You are very kind." She reached up kissed his cheek, squeezing his hand she disappeared inside and unapologetically retired to her corner. He followed her inside rubbing his cheek.

Tibby opened her eyes as Zach quietly asked whether she was up for another trip to the billabong. She smiled as she pulled on her boots. This was a privilege she wasn't going to forgo, even if Amelia was the favoured candidate. They sat on the edge of the platform dangling their feet over the edge making circles in the water with their toes. Tibby yawned and wondered how to ask about his relationship with Amelia. No matter how she thought about it she couldn't introduce the topic in a way that didn't sound petulant, or sour, or malicious. Eventually she said, "I have another question…"

"Hmm. I was thinking it isn't fair that you get all the questions. This morning I have some for you… if that is agreeable?"

"Me? Really?"

"Yeah. I have questions too."

"Oh. I never thought that… that I was terribly interesting," she said mimicking Amelia. He grinned, his eyes crinkling around the edges. She relaxed and laughed; and for a moment she forgot all her fears.

"My first question: when was the moment you knew you wanted to come to Australia?"

"Oh. Well… Let me see. It wasn't all of a sudden. My friend, Winnie, gave me a pamphlet, and we were going to come out together. She was more committed to the idea than me at first. She said this was a place of opportunity, and a way to make our lives better. So, we had it all planned and I went in and got my ticket sorted. And when I told Winnie that I'd done it, she said she didn't believe I would really go through with it, and that she never intended on leaving her family. I felt so betrayed. It was like our friendship meant nothing. Anyway, she stayed, and I left."

He sat for a moment or so, and then asked, "Do you miss your family?"

"My family is not very miss-able. I wish I could talk to my youngest sister most of all. Her name is Janie. She is quiet... and sensitive. If she had been a couple of years older, I would have brought her with me... but she wasn't, and I didn't feel I could wait... so, I just came."

"Is it what you thought it would be? Being here..."

"Being here – at your place? Or Australia?"

"Either..."

"Australia. Well, it's been harder than I ever thought. I had no idea I could be homesick for a family who didn't care... or that I'd miss the drabness of where I lived. Perhaps familiar takes hold of one's heart too... even if has none of the privileges one usually associates with kin."

He noticed she didn't take up the invitation to talk about being at Dellaweir. He let it go. "So, what familiar stuff do you miss most?"

"It is more that there are many strange ways here. It's just working out how to do it differently. Like sewing. I lived in the textile capital of the Empire. My mistress was a well-known seamstress, and she could get any type of fabric she wanted... satins and silks and velvets. She turned out magnificent clothes for important people. Here, I work with plain-weave. It has taken some getting used to, but now I love it. The idea of bush dyes is very different to what a finishing factory can produce, but it has been so much fun doing it myself. Not sure Heather realises these things were done especially for her."

"I think it has by-passed her notice completely. Does it bother you that she has no idea how hard you worked?"

"Me? I am more annoyed that she accused you of making no effort! A whole house! With furniture!"

"Hmm. I'm no longer upset by Heather's blinkers. Who cares if she despises the basic life we live?"

"I'll agree not to care about her pouting if you aren't upset by it." Tibby smiled and stuck out her hand to shake on it. He took her hand and willed himself to keep his touch business-like firm. "Still, just sometimes, I would like Heather to appreciate something," she added wistfully.

"Me too. But some things may not be possible, no matter how much we want them."

She looked away. Did he say that to remind her that no matter how much she wanted this, it would not be possible? He stood up and went to work.

✤

Tibby walked past the fire pit in the cookout area and heard Heather in the bedroom, speaking firmly with Amelia. "... be interesting and amusing. The rest is assured."

"But Mrs Granger..." and her voice faded in a tremolo.

Tibby quickly put some wood on the fire coals and set the billy. *Mrs Granger?* Heather insisted on the familiar use of her Christian name as a fashionable trend, but in private she remained strictly loyal to traditional protocols. Poor Amelia was not allowed to forget her place. Perhaps that is what Zach meant. All the fighting in the world would not affect any change against the all-pervasive will of his influential sister.

As soon as Zach appeared, Amelia also emerged. She sat down beside Zach on the log as they had a morning cup of tea. Zach moved across to accommodate her and she shuffled closer. She hovered over his arm as they cooked eggs and toasted damper. She snatched the towel from Tibby as they began washing up over the basin that was still balancing on an upturned box. Zach watched grimly as Tibby made a very solid effort to say nothing. He slowly turned towards Amelia and said without smiling, "Thank you for being so willing to help. Living in the bush is hard work. Still, there is no obligation for visitors to help with the dishes."

"Oh, but I want to! It is so..."

"...interesting," said Tibby under her breath.

Zach didn't blink, but a definite line of amusement hovered around the sun creases in the corner of his eyes. "Tibby, isn't this refreshing? The mark of a helpful woman." Amelia blushed prettily. "Tibby, will you finish up for me? I have some springers in the paddock I have to check." And he threw her the dishcloth and escaped as a man fleeing a burning building. Tibby deftly caught the cloth and slowly attended to the remaining dishes mutely. Amelia hardly kept an eye on her task, straining her neck to try and catch a glimpse of Zach saddling his horse in the yards. They called them stables, but they really didn't qualify as a structure that substantial.

When he returned from the back paddock, Zach went about tending the animals. He turned around and Amelia was standing there like a ghost, haunting his every move. He jolted. He nodded mutely and went back to the chaff that he was spreading in the feed troughs. He handed her a shovel, and then grabbed another and started to muck out the stable. Zach was keeping his horse stabled for a while so that the pile that collected in the stall could be used for the vege garden. Then they spent time digging garden beds with the collected horse manure. The meaning of self-sufficiency had dramatically changed for Zach. He used to be content with a few potatoes and the odd pumpkin, as long as the chooks were laying. While he was digging, turning and breaking up clods, Amelia sighed contentedly – farm life was so satisfying and she wondered what interesting meals could be made with his produce.

When Zach came back in, Heather spoke abruptly. "Why would you make Amelia do the dishes? It is a despicable show of commonness that is beneath us, Zachary. And you... you should know better! We are here as your guests."

"Of course, but Amelia insisted, even when I did object. So, what could I do? I did commend her usefulness though. She even helped muck out the stables today. And then we dug it into the vege plot; they'll be ready for planting soon. I think Amelia appreciates the bush is a great leveller. Something you will no doubt come to appreciate as well Sister-dear."

"Really Zachary! You push the limits. The stables! Digging in the dirt!"

"It's a 'all-hands-on-deck life' out here. The longer you stay, the dirtier I'd expect your genteel hands will get. I'm starting on the cookhouse soon. Making mudbricks. That should be diverting, Amelia. You might find brick making interesting."

Amelia blushed bright pink and dropped her head. "Oh yes, it does sound interesting."

"Oh Amelia!" exclaimed Heather in disgust. "Really!"

"But you said..."

"Yes but mucking out stables and making bricks out of mud is beyond bounds! Please don't forget whom you came with. Truly!"

"Oh, I could never forget you, Mrs Gr... Miss Heather."

Tibby was awake before Zach even stirred that morning. She'd been lying there... listening to his regular breathing, looking at his face relaxed in sleep. How could she live here with the disappointment of seeing him entrapped by his sister? Should she go? She didn't think Zach disliked Amelia. She wasn't convinced Amelia loved him either. From what she could see, Amelia was just bullied into doing whatever Heather deemed fitting. Tibby had already decided that Zach deserved to be loved. But how she could show him that she was that person? She loved him. If he decided in favour of Heather's expectations, that would be his choice and her cue.

He opened his eyes and for a moment their eyes connected. He couldn't remember not being the first one awake before. Tibby quickly looked away, scrambling for her wrap as she went to the outhouse.

They sat together on the platform at the lagoon in the morning light, Zach looked out across the water. "I'd like to show you something," he said after a while. She glanced at him expectantly as he pulled out a folded piece of brown paper, saved from the parcels of calico brought from town. She pushed down her disappointment and took the sheet.

"I wanted your opinion on this. What do you think?"

It was a simple drawing of the cookhouse, and he was keen to talk about his plan. "The current setup was only temporary..."

That made her smile... "Eight years temporary..."

"Anything is temporary when it's not permanent," he said pointing to the diagram. "I'll use bricks behind the open hearth... and the chimney to vent the smoke away. I'm thinking about setting a proper oven on this side. I'll extend the sidewalls out here to protect the fireplace from the winds that mainly come from this direction. Hooks here to hang pots from the rafters... covered roof out to here. Will use the bricks instead of cobblestone for the courtyard because that will be simpler, I think. What do you reckon? Dry, shaded and no mud. Thought that's got to be an improvement."

"What about a pantry? Or a meat house?"

"Hmm. Well..." He studied it for a while. "I guess... we can make a room with shelves and hooks for pantry storage. Will have to make it possum proof. Good point."

"A table?"

"We have a table inside."

"But a place for preparing meals... and washing up. It would be easier... save taking it inside and out again. Just an idea..." she said apologetically. There was that nagging doubt again... that he didn't take her ideas seriously.

He grinned. "See. This was a test to see if you would pick that up."

"Hardly! You forgot about it completely." She laughed at him.

He spread the map out again. "How about we extend this wall... and put a bench along here. Set the water bucket lower. Use this protected area to stack the wood."

She felt bolder. "If you make the wall lower... we can see outside to the trees. I've done a lot of my life without trees. That's something different that I like here."

"A half-wall might look unfinished."

"Anything is finished... when it is finished," she said in mock seriousness. "It would be better than standing there looking into a brick wall."

He shrugged. "Can't refute my own logic, can I?"

"Well, you did ask..."

"I asked because you are my consultant in all matters domestic. It is improved. Thank you."

She smiled and thought for a moment life was wonderful. And he got up and started filling the drum to take back to the house.

As Zach came inside, Heather strolled in through the bedroom door, holding a card. "You've been holding out on me Little Brother."

"In what way?"

"We have been invited to a dinner at your neighbour's. Saturday night. Not much notice. Thank goodness! I don't think I could wait for the usual amount of time. Social engagements around here are so scarce I feel positively cloistered. Who thought I would ever live the deprived life of a nun?"

Zach considered a little religious influence might be an improvement. "I didn't take much stock in you being bothered with the invitation. These are not people you know."

"Well, you know me: always willing to meet new acquaintances. I have a tendency to distrust your antisocial ways, Zachary. I wonder what it is you hide."

"It may be nothing more than that I do not find those people interesting enough for my time."

"There is an arrogance in that stance that completely befuddles me, Zachary. You sink your inheritance into this cesspit you call Dellaweir, and then think that you have become some sort of landed gentry, too good for ordinary folk."

That she would accuse him of snobbery was almost too much. "I fear you over-estimate me, Sister. When I said I struggle to find the energy for it, it is not so much arrogance, as tedium. Rather than being perplexed by the lack of interesting, I thought that might be something that you and your friend might recognise," he said with slight twist on his lips.

Tibby came through the door with a basket of laundry. She could feel the tension crackling between them. Zach saw her standing there in her calico skirt and pinafore. "So, Amelia, you're similar in height to Tabitha; is there something you could lend her that would be suitable for a dinner invitation with our social neighbours?"

Heather turned around. "If she has nothing suitable to wear, she may prefer to stay home."

"If we are going; we are *all* going," he said with the finality of a full stop.

Heather looked at him briefly and turned to Amelia. "The pale green might fit her. I think the lemon highlights your hair, so you can wear that. And if we add those ribbons, I think it will be very flattering." They disappeared to talk dresses, hair, and grooming.

Zach came over and stood awkwardly by Tibby as she plunged into her sewing with a frenzied focus. "We have been invited to dinner at Bates' place. I didn't think they would be inclined; however, it seems Heather is set. Are you okay to come? It is not an exclusive invitation – a Shearer's Festival they put on every year. It used to be a week-long free-for-all, but now it is a more modest affair. He invites important names and the valley landowners. That includes us. I've gone once before."

"Do you want me to go?"

"I have no intention of going if you do not."

"Well, I..." Was he trying to show her in a subtle sort of way that it was time to move on with the original plan? Nothing seemed more unattractive than parading herself like a haunch of meat hanging off a hook at the market stall.

The possibility of Tibby being charmed by other options bothered Zach; and Bates had been first option. One way to fix that would be to closet her, never let her see alternatives. But is ignorance a genuine form of choice? Can you love well when you know nothing else? Heather was right. This place was rather plain and all his plans to upgrade didn't seem enough. Yes, he was curious as to how she would react, fearful almost. "We don't have to go," he said again... almost hopefully.

"Heather would be disappointed."

"Heather would live."

Tibby smiled. "And make your life miserable as she survives her disappointment. I will be okay. We can go."

The green dress needed mending before it could be worn. It looked rather plain when compared to the lemon frills and ribbons adorning Amelia, and Heather's parade of her ivory lace ruffles overlaying ruched purple. "I always wear the colour of Scottish heather when going out. It is my namesake after all, and it is my most becoming look." When Tibby tried on her dress, Heather looked her up and down, and sanctioned approval due to its plainness. "You know, Amelia, this dress is very suitable for Tabitha. Why don't we give it to her?"

"Oh yes, Ma'am. It would be my pleasure." Tibby saw a genuine earnestness in Amelia's eyes and thanked her.

What Heather hadn't taken into consideration was Tibby's sewing experience with a Master Seamstress. She retrieved from her bag some ribbons Zach had provided on various shopping expeditions, and when she embroidered around the torn neckline and frayed sleeves, it went from drab to discreetly flattering.

Zach went down to the lagoon to bathe and let the women have the run of the hut to get ready. He hung a small mirror on a nail in the tethering post, and after sharpening his razor on the leather strap, had a shave. Then he sat there for a long while, wondering if this was the time Tibby would stretch her wings, like a wounded eaglet he had once nursed. Then remembered the instant that fledgling Wedgetail flew up, healed and strong, and found the currents. It had been a most exhilarating moment. But the thought that Tabitha might fly free and out of his life stabbed like a knife in his chest. He put on his boots, slung his only 'going out' jacket over his shoulder and walked up to the house. He had resolved on one thing at least.

When he came inside, Tabitha turned and blinked. Zach stood there in a suit. It was a modest cut, but he looked the proper gentleman. She had never seen Zach in anything other than his work breeches or town-trousers. Without saying anything he went over the chest under the window and took out a small box. He opened it and picked out a small pouch. He walked over to Tibby and placed a small oval cameo in her hand, the sage green backing matched her dress. "This belonged to my mother. I would like you to wear this tonight if you would not mind." He adjusted it at her neck.

Heather turned around and gasped. "Zachary! You wouldn't!"

"I would and I have."

'You can't give it to *her*!"

"It is on loan to wear tonight. You are both adorned like peacocks, and this piece suits Tabitha's simple outfit."

"Well, since you put it like that..." said Heather disparagingly.

He turned to Tibby and said, "You look beautiful." He held her in his eyes for a moment. "I am charged to pass this on to my daughter, so I really am not at liberty to gift it to anyone just yet..." He was quietly disappointed in himself. He *had* meant it to be a gift. Heather had got to him once more. When would he stand up to her?

Tibby placed her hand over her neck and felt the coolness of the pendant under her palm. A ripple of heat ran through her body. It felt like her dream. It also felt like she would wake up and it wouldn't be real... again. "Are you sure?"

Oh, he was sure. She was standing there bashful and completely unaware how beautiful she was. He turned away, in case he embarrassed himself by kissing her... and simply said, "Yes," and walked to the cart, hitched to the horse, readied for their social outing.

No fine carriages or comfortable sulkies, and the only ease offered was a couple of blankets thrown over the storage boxes on the back that doubled as seats, to prevent their going-out dresses snagging on the rough wood panels.

They crossed the creek down-stream at a culvert and passed a collection of rag-tag huts. Heather looked on in perturbed silence, as wide eyes gawked back at them passing. She had assumed from the quality of invitation stationery that someone with a little bit of social savvy had sent it. She was mortified to think they could be turning up to a hut the size of Zachary's, dressed for proper society. Perhaps Zachary had been quite sincere about her level of disinterest in this social event. She considered feigning illness and demanding that Zachary return home.

The line of huts finished, and Zach nodded to a couple of stockmen as they drove along the track beside the stockyards. He pulled up beside the stables out the back of the homestead and jumped down. He offered Tibby, who was riding right at the back, his hand, then Heather and Amelia. They stepped into a large yard with shade trees and ornamental shrubs. Garden beds ran along the footpaths to the homestead. When they came around the side to the front of the house there were rows of parked buggies, carts and even an occasional carriage. Heather allowed a feathery laugh escape, giddy in relief. "Where did these all come from? We didn't pass a single one."

"Quicker for us to come the back-way. Redwood is the biggest spread in the valley. They generally enjoy showing off. They usually have another shindig after shearing."

"Prominent family. Pleasant aspect. You did well to accept this invitation, Zachary." The night did bode very well after all, and she was anxious to meet the mistress of such an establishment.

He grunted. He didn't RSVP anything.

Tibby on the other hand became more subdued in her confusion. This was the home of Bates? It was intended that she be introduced to this man? This picture did not match the one she had in her head. Zach had not said much, but what he had confided had caused her to imagine squalor and cruelty and bellowing... not unlike her childhood home. Had he been falsely defamatory, so that she would not come here? Was this manipulation so that she would not have the opportunity to better her position? Every day of that insufferable journey on the ship... she had imagined something better, barely surviving on a fragile fragment of hope.

Amelia became very attached to Heather's side. She smoothed her dress and adjusted her gloves and fiddled with her ribbons. Heather took her arm and serenely walked up the front stairs, as she quietly reminded Amelia under her breath to "calmly take command of herself".

Zach reached out to escort Tibby through the door, but she stepped aside. At the door he paused and introduced his sister and her friend to the hostess, Mrs Novak. She was a mature woman with a severe brow. "And this is Tabitha, a family friend." She bobbed a curtsy and walked inside. The number of ladies in the room was not large, so the arrival of three unfamiliar beautiful women so handsomely dressed caused quite a pause in the clusters of conversation around the room. Heather glowed and curtsied with such social ease that she made quite an impression.

Heather quickly took in the style and quality of the furnishings and draperies. It was one telling way to determine the social suitability of a family. What a contrast to the rustic simplicity of Dellaweir! Everything she saw pleased her. Zach led her to a cluster of gentlemen in the middle of the room. A solidly built man in a handsome brocade vest and matching waistcoat turned to meet them. He eyed the women carefully and lingered over Heather's beautiful gown and fine full figure.

"Logan! Good of you to come. All on the level here at Redwood Park. Everyone welcome."

Zach nodded and said nothing. Tibby flinched and quickly looked at Zach who ignored the blatant condescension. She expected Heather to rile up. Instead, she just smiled gloriously, and curtsied. "I completely agree, Sir, unless we make allowances none of us would ever step outside our parlour rooms. I think the fresh air and company does us good and our..."

Bates smiled, fascinated that, as she prattled on in meaningless social banter, she bypassed his slur against their party's lower status. Rather than making her seem a little dim-witted, he had the impression he was in the presence of an authentic lady who really felt the relief of appropriate social company.

Zach left them for a moment and did a circuit of the room, nodding, offering a greeting or a short social courtesy. He came back and stood with Tibby, who had retreated by the wall, trying to disappear into the panelling. "Well. That's done. I should be able to stand out of the way for the rest of the evening... and try and outlast Heather's insatiable thirst for conversation."

"You don't enjoy these types of things?"

"Not much. You will remember I told Heather I find them boring. I wasn't exaggerating. Everyone comes here to impress, and they end up embarrassing themselves in one way or another."

Tibby looked around the room. She smiled to herself and thought ironically that as a seamstress she would recognise people by their clothes rather than their names or faces. Mrs Novak was the lady in the navy-blue hat with feathers. Bates was wearing that brocade waistcoat. He was talking rather animatedly with a man in a brown double-breasted tailored jacket. So, this was Bates: the man on her paperwork. She looked at him with the same kind of curiosity she had when she used to watch the factory bosses and foremen drive past in their carriages as she walked to work. It was like looking through shop windows without a penny in your pocket.

Zach noticed her keen observation. He couldn't let it pass. "So, this is what I saved you from. Any inclination to try and wile your way in here after all?" He looked around the room of faces. "I wonder for whom you were intended?"

Tibby was flooded with relief. If she missed this because she nearly died, twice, even such a high price seemed fair. She felt removed, like they were porcelain figurines gracing a display cabinet. Odd that she could appreciate the occasion without regret. "It doesn't look so bad. It certainly seems to offer a level of comfort." Tibby knew it wasn't comfort that was after now. She aimed higher.

"Easy and cheap," Zach grunted.

"I'm trying to think what disadvantages this position might have. I haven't come up with many... any." It was true: on paper this position read far superior to the one she had. But she knew the reality of it. It was not better.

He grunted again, unhappy with her candid summation. He didn't want her to be dissatisfied with his place. With him. He needed to defend his choices, his place, his work. What right did she have to judge? Certainly, Heather and her snobby disdain was predicably critical, but he never expected Tibby to be infected with that. He carefully regulated his breathing and turned away. "I'm going out to get some fresh air. It's a bit stuffy in here."

He stalked off, and she watched him go. She knew he was cranky with her, but what right did he have to carry on? One word and he would have her forever. That's all it would take... but no, he couldn't, wouldn't do that. She looked out over the room again. Heather was chatting vivaciously with Mrs Novak and some other women, and Amelia was hovering like a butterfly around nectar. The man in the brown double-breasted jacket, talking with Bates, twitched his whiskers. His shaved upper lip smiled at Tibby encouragingly. She bobbed her head to cover a grin. He looked ridiculous! She gathered her manners and curtsied politely and hurried out to find Zach.

A maid rushed past, her cap ruffled and her apron screwed. "I don't suppose you know where...?" asked Tibby tentatively looking around the grounds a little disorientated. The maid quickly smoothed her hair, and barely paused. She nodded back into dark towards the stables. Oh. Of course, he would wait by the cart.

Tibby glanced back over her shoulder at her retreating figure and appreciated that Zach never made her feel like the help. What they did, they did together. She hadn't meant to offend him, but her observations had really been just to note, how this position with all its perceived advantages, was not her choice. She sighed and started to walk towards the stables. She wanted to say... she wanted... well, a lot of things. But lately she was increasingly confused about their relationship. In some ways they were closer, and in others, still total strangers. Why wasn't it simple... all straight across the board? Why were there times when everything was guarded... and other times it felt incredibly connected?

She felt the pendant around her neck and touched the raised relief of the figurine under her fingers. His gesture held huge trust, even in the face of Heather's disapproval. That was something else she noticed. His sister's control was quite constricting and yet on a couple of note-worthy occasions he had gone directly against his sister's wishes. Like the sleeping arrangements... and this pendent that rested between her fingers. He wasn't moved on either of those occasions.

Oh.

It was like a light glowed in her mind. She stopped as the realisation expanded and brightened like the dawn light over the surface of the billabong. He defended her place in his home because he saw it as her home too. He never allowed Heather to cross that line with her. Tibby was not a visitor, as Heather was. Or Amelia. She was home.

Suddenly she wanted to be with him, to reassure him that she understood. She knew there was still stuff to work out, but just now she needed him to know that all of the luxuries of this place meant nothing compared to the prospect of being home.

She gathered up her skirts and hurried off towards the stables. "Ma'am!" She paused and turned around. "Ma'am?" The man in the brown double-breasted jacket hurried to her side. He smiled again and his shaved upper lip sort of curled, twitching his sideburn whiskers.

"I'm sorry, do you need something?" she asked.

"I need... something indeed..."

"Pardon? Excuse me Sir; I have never met you before. What can you mean?"

"Back in the room... you were watching me."

"Oh? Ah, you are the man talking with Mr Bates. In truth, I was looking at the company in general."

"Then you curtsied and invited me to follow..."

"What?" She looked at him confused. "I curtsied because you smiled at me. I was trying to be mannerly."

He stepped forward and she stepped back. "You wanted me to follow..." His meaning began to emerge, like a snake peeking his head out of a hole.

"You are mistaken, Sir. I didn't! Excuse me, I have to go." She turned and fled. The brown coat caught her in a second. She started to panic. "Zach! Zach! Where are you?"

The man grabbed her sleeve and pulled her up to his side. She screamed and he slapped her mouth with his hand. "You started this. What is mannerly is to finish it," he said.

She thrashed and fought and was not going to stop. She felt her head spinning as his hand clamped over her mouth and nose. She couldn't breathe. Lantern lights seemed to bob and then started turning dark and still she lashed out. She was pushed to the ground, the noise in her head drowned out everything as she screamed and screamed. It was happening again.

Gradually she became aware of the shouting fading... an eerie stillness filled its place. No one was grabbing at her. She was thrashing alone. She tried to edge away, opening her eyes a lantern swung in the periphery of her vision. She tried to focus, and she realised there was blood on her face, in her eyes, sticky and blurring her vision. She sat up and wiped her face with the heel of her hand. The lantern came closer and she backed away, scrambling in her fear.

The light glowed on Zach's face and spoke gently, his lip bleeding. "Tibby... he's gone. They've gone. I'm here. It's Zach." His mouth was pressed tightly together in constrained anger.

Something about his tone sounded so familiar, like a soothing dream that was being relived... a dream of being cared for, gently, firmly, patiently, being restored back to health. She let out a breath, shuddering in horror. He was by her side in a second.

"I should not have left. I should have stayed. I'm sorry." His voice cracked in contrition.

"He said... he said that I..." she gasped, and her dry eyes reflected the trembling revulsion that ran through her being. "I never... I didn't!"

"Shh... I know. Can you stand? Are you hurt bad?"

She didn't want the awareness of her body to return. Sensation was too frightening to acknowledge. "I'm bleeding... I don't know..." He helped her to her feet.

He brushed her face with his kerchief. It didn't really hurt though. "Don't think the blood is yours. It's on your dress though. Sorry."

"Not mine? I'm okay?"

"Can't see any cuts." He held her has they made their way across the dusty courtyard to the cart. Some men from the stables looked and sneered, and she could almost hear Zach growl, like a dog baring his teeth in warning. But she didn't mind. She just wanted to go; to get away. "But we have to wait for Heather. We can't..."

"If you want to go home, I can come back for Heather."

"I... please no. Maybe we could go somewhere and wait a bit. But I don't want to be alone. Please. Not even at home."

"Sure. We'll go where there is space. I'm not leaving you. You won't be alone."

He grabbed the blanket off the back and wrapped it around her shoulders. She sat beside him as he drove the cart out along the track, and he pulled off into a side paddock. He spread the other rug on the grass. "Here... let's just wait here."

She sat. Close. She didn't wait to be invited. She didn't wait for his permission. She closed her eyes and then opened them and looked up into the night sky smeared with stars. "You said the blood is not mine. What happened?"

"His nose bled some. May have lost a tooth. I don't think you are cut." He wiped her face again as if to reassure himself.

She shuddered and moved closer. He took off his jacket and wrapped it around her shoulders. Then readjusted the blanket around both of them, cocooning her safely under his arm.

"I was coming to find you. I needed to tell you something. He followed me. He was saying...

He looked at her, in the faded light of the lantern that was hanging off the side of the cart. He said nothing and figured if it was important, she would keep going.

"... he said I wanted... He said I asked him to come. I only curtsied because I was trying to be mannerly because they are fancy people. He thought I wanted him to follow me."

Zach grimaced and felt his anger seethe. A world where a curtsy was an invitation for a roll in the hay was about as base as it gets. Every bias he held about this place was confirmed in his mind. "I'll remember a curtsy is just a curtsy."

"I didn't thank you for coming quickly. Thank you..."

He responded with a squeeze to her shoulder.

Tibby turned to him. "I'm sorry you were angry with me. I didn't want that. That's what I came to tell you. I wanted you to tell you that I don't care for their music or their upholstered chairs or their pretty tablecloths. I wanted you to know that." She swallowed. What if this wasn't what he wanted to hear? She swallowed again and ploughed on. "I needed to tell you that Dellaweir feels like home. Not this place. I want to stay at home with you."

"You said it had advantages."

"Yes... but all those advantages don't feel like home. You do."

"Me?"

She nodded in the dark, and looked at the sky, and tried very hard not to cry.

She heard him let out a sigh, and she wasn't sure if it was relief, or weariness, or impatience. But he didn't move away... and he didn't say anything further for a long while.

"I'm sorry you had to come tonight. I could have sent the invitation back. I didn't want to come; I know what they are like here. I should have stuck to my guns."

"Heather's having a good time."

"Heather's a snob. You're not like her."

"You don't like her much, do you?"

"Just can't please her..."

"But she's family..."

"Yep. Doesn't mean I have to like her. You feel more like family than she ever will. You know I don't really want to talk about Heather. I'm glad it feels like home for you though. I like that you think that."

"You do? I was thinking how you... well... draw a line with her. It's like you understand that she's the visitor and I'm not. That's what I wanted to say. That's why I left the party to find you."

He shifted his weight and turned to face her in the dark. "Can I tell you something?"

"Sure..."

"It never actually believed Heather would come. I never expected she would say yes. I thought you needed more time, and I didn't want you to go. But I didn't know how to say that... because you were still not strong. So, I made up this idea that I needed some help getting the house ready for someone. But then you were so into it... and did so many beautiful things that I felt I needed to make it legitimate. I was so sure she wouldn't even answer my letter that I didn't hesitate to write and ask her. I thought that even if she did respond, which was unlikely, she would never come here. So, when that letter came, I never hesitated to give it to you to read because I was so sure it would say she couldn't make the trip. But she said she was coming. I was shocked. I really didn't expect that. And if that wasn't enough, then she turned up with Amelia. Well, it's all backfired. All I wanted was for you to stay."

"You could've just asked me."

"Wasn't real sure how to do that. Didn't know you quite like I do now. If it was now, it would have been easier."

"Easier for what?"

"Easier to ask..."

"But you still haven't..."

"What?"

"You still haven't asked me to stay…"

"Will you then?"

"Why?"

"Because I want…" He cleared his throat. He knew he needed to declare himself. "My hut is just a hut without you. I want you home too. Like you said."

"So, this is still about the hut?'

"No, it's about you and me. Me. I want you to stay."

"For how long?"

"What do you mean how long? Have you somewhere else to be?"

"Depends on how long I guess."

"Is forever, okay?"

She smiled into the dark. "Okay with me."

"Good."

"What will Heather say?"

"You talk about my sister excessively. I really don't care what Heather has to say about this. Which will be plenty I guess," he said with a grimace. He was silent for a while considering something. "Tabitha…?"

"Yes?"

"Does this mean you will marry me?"

"Depends…"

"On what?"

"On whether you ask…"

"Oh. Right. I'll keep that in mind then."

Damn. He wasn't going to ask. Maybe. Not yet. Maybe not ever. She was suitable as a companion, but perhaps not suitable as a wife. Afterall she was one who had been attacked, molested, despoiled, pregnant. Well, she knew in spite of all this, she had a home... and home was safe. For now, that was enough.

"Tabitha...?"

"Yes?"

"Can I kiss you?"

She jumped a little and felt the back of her throat stiffened, all the way down her spine and she held her breath. She hadn't realised that this would be a problem for her. If a kiss terrified her, why was she so keen to get married? How would she ever do that? "Umm... I guess..."

Zach held her hand and lifted it to his lips and kissed the back of it gently. "Thank you," he said. "I'm glad you are home."

She felt her body relax. He was more the gentleman than that dining room full of vests and jackets. "I am too..." Then she remembered he'd knocked a tooth out for her and felt her face flush in a self-conscious blush. She was grateful the lantern light was low and put her hand to her throat to cover her embarrassment even under the refuge of the shadows.

She stopped and gasped. "Oh Zach! Zach!" She scrambled to her feet. "The cameo! It's gone! Your mother's necklace. Oh, I'm so sorry! It's gone."

16.

"Check the blanket..." She knelt as Zach held the lantern for her and she carefully felt along the folds of her dress, and the blanket and his jacket. She retraced her steps back towards the cart. He lifted the lantern high and ran his hand along the floor below the front seat. "We may have to come back in daylight. I'll mark the spot with a stake..." He pulled a wooden picket out of the boxes on the cart and banged it in with a mallet. "It'll give us a general idea." He paused. "We have to go and pick up Heather soon. We'll have a look where you fell over while we are there."

She looked at him. "I didn't fall over, I was pushed... and..." She shuddered, took a deep breath, and braced herself.

"Oh. Of course. You won't want to go back there..." He chided himself for the obvious. Idiot!

She heard his voice change. Would he really respect that she may not feel up to it? That was kindness she didn't expect. "No, we can go. We have to find it."

"We'll try. I guess it wasn't worth that much, as far as trinkets go..."

"But it was your mother's! That is irreplaceable. As I was walking down to the stables, I was thinking how elegant it felt, and how you trusted me to wear it. I'm so sorry. I've broken your trust."

"The chain was broken, not my trust. You didn't mean this to happen."

"Maybe someone has picked it up."

"Maybe not... If we're lucky it'll be on the ground." and it sounded like he definitely thought this was the preferred option.

She stayed close to his side as the lantern light cast a rather eerie sort of swirl of light over the ground. She tried to ignore the numerous eyes from the stable that gathered to watch their search. She leant over with a leap as something glinted... and picked up a button. She checked her sleeves and found one missing. They had the right spot, but there was no locket.

"Let's go home," said Zach. "We've done all we can for now. I'll mention to the housekeeper there's a few quid for its return."

Heather chatted amiably on the way back about her complete satisfaction with the suitability of the neighbours, and how genteel company was such an invigorating change. "There was a girl there... nice little thing... wife of the head stockman, the overseer... really hit it off with Amelia. It would be so appropriate for her to keep up the company. I've organised to come back and have tea."

Tibby hoped this meant that the pressure on their domestic arrangement might be relieved a little now that this bright shining social situation had appeared. What a most peculiar evening! What an array of stark contrasts: personal revelation and misunderstanding; violation and protection; intimate trust and tragic misfortune. She felt a strange sense of relief, as she stepped onto the verandah, regarding Heather's newfound distraction. She wished and she prayed that the cameo would be found, then all would be good with the world.

Tibby jolted as she felt a hand on her arm. She froze and opened her eyes. "Shh... time to get the watercart," she heard him whisper

She struggled out of sleep and pulled on her boots and coat. The mornings were darker with the changing season, and cooler. He opened the gate for her, and she walked through, rubbing her eyes in sleep. Zach always did mornings with such ease. For her it was harder. She stumbled a little on a loose stone and he caught her with his arm. Without saying anything for a moment he held her steady. "You right?"

"Hmm... still asleep I think."

It took a while for her to notice he was still holding her. She looked up at him and he released the pressure. "Take it easy. Bob can't carry you back once the water barrel is full."

She was doused in fatigue, trying to stir herself to wakefulness, "I'm going to have to learn to do mornings better. Seems farm-life deems it necessary."

"Necessary? I've done this by myself for so long I deem having you along is a bonus."

She smiled at the flattery. There it was again... how he made her feel like being home. But was it enough to marry?

"Heather and Amelia are going back to Redwood Park tomorrow. They've asked me to go with them. But I'd rather not..."

"Don't go then. You don't have to."

"Well... two things. They asked me... and they don't usually include me... and I thought I might be able to ask around and see if anyone found the cameo."

They sipped tea in the spacious parlour to the great satisfaction of Heather. There was a rather eclectic gathering of connections, hosted by Bates' aunt, Mrs Novak. It was generally understood that she would always hold matriarchal status at Redwood Park even when her nephew settled on a new wife. Bates' comfortable homestead, his eligibility as widower and his influential position, had many women in the region seeking an opportunity to present themselves. But of all the potential brides that came through the gate, he had not made a choice. Heather was talking with the wife from a neighbouring property in the valley – Mrs Leybourne, who was accompanied by her eldest daughter, Leala, who as a young teenager was comfortably enjoying the adult women's circle. The cousin of the schoolmaster was having a tete-a-tete with the constable's sister-in-law; and Tibby sat beside the daughter of the Postmaster come general merchant who was chitchatting with Amelia about the quality of the biscuits.

Heather didn't even seem to notice that the most-suitable, waited-for overseer's wife, who had prompted accepting this invitation, had not arrived. When her apologies were frankly relayed by the housekeeper, no one seemed troubled or even disappointed. The windows opened up onto the verandah, and they could see the coming and goings of station life with a sort of fishbowl detachment. Gardeners gawked as they walked past with hoes or pitchforks across their shoulders. Mrs Novak had a word with the housekeeper who diverted the workers out of their proximity. The refreshments were agreeable, the conversation suitably bland and meaningless, and the cooler weather meant their comfort was not bothered by too many flies. The occasional feathered fan brushed them away. Amelia thought these were an ingenious alternative to expensive silk fans and began to prattle her enthusiasm to anyone who was not rude enough to turn away. Then she shared an inspired idea of making a fan out of feathers gathered from the chook run.

Through all this Tibby felt removed and very much out of place. She realised she would have been far more comfortable sitting with housekeeping, mending socks. Still, she sat through the proceedings patiently, waiting for a moment when she might be able to mention the lost pendent. Eventually she described it to the post-master's daughter when Amelia was called upon to sing. She took advantage of the pause while they were sitting together waiting for the item to start and there were no more biscuits to discuss. Other than that, she had no opportunity and felt the whole afternoon was a waste and would have been better employed working on her patchwork project at home.

Amelia sang a pretty, but certainly not a very artistic vocal piece. Heather realised that music was not well understood or appreciated, and a pub ditty would have sufficed just as well. She felt suitably superior, and declared she was gratified that she could offer the services of Amelia to elevate the culture of the occasion. As they were leaving, Mrs Novak slipped Heather a card, and took her hand warmly. Heather discreetly inserted it in her sleeve and smiled her cordial farewells.

"Did you enjoy playing ladies?" Zach asked as they walked down to the waterhole the next morning.

Tibby grimaced. The whole proceeding was self-inflicted. "In truth, I was bored. All I wanted was to see if someone had found the locket, but I really didn't get an opportunity to ask around. I'm sorry it has not been found. My lesson is learnt – I will not feel obliged when your sister speaks again.”

“I trust it was not just because you know I don’t like these types of things that you felt you could not enjoy yourself.”

“I was bored mostly because I was thinking of all the things I could be doing here; not because I thought you expected me to be.”

“Good. I want you to be able to enjoy the things you prefer.”

She smiled. Did he know? “I prefer this, and not just because you expect it.”

He grinned in return. “Shame you hold no weight for my opinion then, because I would be inclined to tell you that I am pleased you enjoy my company.”

“Not Amelia?”

“Amelia? Here? Now?” He looked at her with a wry twist on his lips. “Seriously?”

“Yes... well wouldn’t you prefer her to be here?” She looked away.

“Don’t ever remember asking her along even when she was less then subtle in suggesting she be invited.”

“See... she wants to come.”

“Of course. Desperately. She wants me to fall in love with her.”

She never expected him to be so frank. She looked at him quickly. “It sounds like you expect she will be disappointed. Poor Amelia.”

"Amelia will be happy as long as Heather is happy. She's pretty and compliant. It shouldn't be too hard to place her in someone's bed."

"Zachary!"

"It's true. She'll be fine. They will find someone else; I am sure. I do not need to feel bad that I don't want to marry her."

"You don't?"

"Heather may have me marked as her husband, but my interests are elsewhere. So, in this my sister will not get her way."

Tibby went silent. Her heart beating. She wanted to believe that there was a possibility... but she felt so unworthy that she immediately deemed it implausible. There was probably some other love that she didn't know about. He did go to town regularly.

"Tibby? Now is not the time *not* to be curious. I want you to ask about this. Please."

"But I don't want to hear that you love someone else!"

Now he was confused. "You want me to be with Amelia? Sorry to disappoint. That is not going to happen. The woman is dense. I have more meaningful conversations with my horse."

She laughed at him. "I thought she was interesting."

"Then I'm worried by your definition of interesting."

"Is there someone else?"

"Of course, there is. I can't understand that you don't know that."

"How can I know? I never see anyone else come here. It didn't seem like you were interested in women at all until I came... and now you have suitors lining up."

"They can line up into town for all I care. My heart is taken. That is the mystery of it. She seems unaware... and that makes this so frustrating."

"I don't understand. If you love someone, how could she not know that?" Tears filled her eyes. She was too late. If she had been strong, it might have been different, but he had just confirmed that his heart was taken. She knew then that she would have to go. She could not do this. She would not do it. But she would not go to Bates' place. That was too close. She might work to save up and go back home. As far away as possible.

"I have no idea. But she does not seem to have a trace of suspicion. And it is not like I don't give hints. Perhaps... since you advise me on matters domestic... what do you think I should do?"

Tibby looked pained. Really? He wanted advice on how to declare himself? No way would she help him do that! She closed her eyes and regulated her breathing. She could not.

He took her hand. "Please Tibby. Help me out here. You are my friend. You know what to do."

She quickly removed her hand and shook her head violently. "I can't Zach. I can't. Really."

"Why not? I am asking very civilly. You did agree to advise me on matters domestic... for board and lodging."

"That is not fair."

He shrugged... and tried not to smile.

She closed her eyes again. "If it was me..." She stalled.

"Yes?"

She regulated her breathing and tried again. "If it was me... I would just like to be told outright. No hints. No riddles. No assumptions. Just declare yourself. Plain like..."

"That doesn't sound very romantic. Don't women prefer romance?"

She shrugged. "It's not romantic to be uncertain of one's intentions. I would rather know... and then explore the romance in the knowing and the confidence of being certain one is loved."

"Hmm. That makes sense. How would I make such a declaration?"

"Oh, come on!"

"Truly. What would I say?"

"I don't know... Well perhaps you could try... "*I love you.*" That would cover it."

"Just... I love you?"

"Sure."

"Well how? Do I hold her hand? Like this?" He reached out and took her hand again. She flinched... but didn't move. "Should I be close or far away?"

"I think that would depend. Closer perhaps if you love her much."

"Like this?" He moved closer. "Or this?" and he leant in even closer.

She closed her eyes and saw the imprint of his body in the moonlight lying on his swag. She swallowed and squeezed her eyes tighter. She so desperately wanted this to be real. Last time she woke it had just been a dream.

"You are laughing at me."

"Not at all. I am very serious about getting this right. She needs to know that I love her more than any other woman on the face of creation. That she can be certain of my love. That I will never look at another woman, no matter how suitable my sister thinks she is. She needs to know I love *her*."

"Oh Zach..." Tears filled her eyes. "I wish..." She tried to pull away. This was too hard.

"Tibby. Look at me. Look. Tabitha... I love you. *You*. I am not practicing this for any other person. This is for you. I love you. I want *you* to be my wife. Will you marry me?"

"Me?"

"I love you. You."

"Me?"

"That's what I said. You know it is true. I love you. Ever since you landed on my porch, I have been terrified you would be taken from me, or leave, or die. Which you have tried a couple of times by the way. Please marry me."

"But you said you would be embarrassed to be married to me."

"I never said that."

"You did. When Heather arrived."

"Well, I might have said that if Heather was embarrassed by my choice of bride that is no concern of mine."

"You wanted me to chaperone you and Amelia."

"I wanted to be sure I was not left alone with her. I needed you to see I was not flirting with her."

"Actually, I thought you were quite rude."

"I am of the opinion that Amelia is a person with which subtle does not work. And you were jealous. Just a little bit. It must mean you care."

"I have been here so long, and you have never seemed interested. Why now?"

"I am interested. All the way. But you were hurt and scared, and I didn't want to hurt or scare you more. I wasn't going to rush this. I needed you to know you could trust me. At least that was the plan." He shook his head as if amazed. How many times had he been on the verge of declaring himself and held back... because he was being careful. And she thought he was reluctant!

"When you said I could stay... you wouldn't ask me to marry me then. I thought it was because of what happened to me. Suitable as a companion, but not as a wife."

"Not suitable? Oh Tibby. It amazes me how right this is. I thought I was giving obvious signals that you would one day be my wife. I can't believe that these are the things that have made you doubt! And then you said I needed to ask; I wondered about that and thought you wanted a proper proposal... like you wanted proper material for your sewing. But I only bought plain-weave. Well perhaps my idea of a proposal is plain as well, so I am asking you now. Plain and clear. Please, will you marry me, Tibby? I love you. I can't get plainer than that."

17.

Tibby basked in the quiet romance of knowing she was loved. "I'm so glad we decided to keep this between us. Having to cope with Heather's disgust would spoil it."

"Heather knows," said Zach quietly.

"But she hasn't said anything..."

"She's spending a lot of time at Redwood Park. She knows her days are numbered here."

"Oh Zach." Suddenly fear gripped Tibby's heart. She had been so confident she didn't know. "She knows?"

"Pretty sure."

"Does this mean she has accepted it... me... us?"

"Wouldn't think so."

"But..." Tibby's mind was swirling. She had been so secure in the silence. But now it just seemed like a cloud of naivety. "How?"

He shrugged. "You are... happy. I am a man in love. These things leak out. Do you realise you hum when you sew?"

Tibby was silent. She stared at the muddy edge around the lagoon and didn't understand why she felt so afraid. "Zach... let's not wait. Let's get married now."

"Okay... can't see any flaws in that plan. I'll go to town tomorrow. I'll see the priest." He leant over and kissed her. She responded almost frantically.

"This seems like I will wake up from a dream and it will never be true."

"Well... get ready to be Mrs Logan. Tomorrow when I return, I will be able tell you when your spinster days are done."

She pulled back and feigned a pout. "You think I accept you just to secure the social distinction of no longer being an unmarried maid?"

His reply was quick and serious. "Can't possibly think it would be anything else. You only get only a plain hut; a sole farmer without workers; limited resources; hard work. In all respects it's not a good offer."

"Zachary Logan... you miss a significant point."

"Oh?"

"A gunya would be sufficient... because no matter what it is like, we are together. So, whatever we start with, we will work to make it better. See what we have done since I arrived... and that was for visitors, not even for us."

He smiled. "It was always for us."

"A secret I was never privy to."

"And now?"

"Oh yes. Now. You may not consider it a good offer... but for me it is beyond my wildest expectations. I never expected love."

He laughed. "Perhaps it is to my advantage then, that you are not ambitious... and this is enough."

"You are enough. You. I want for nothing else."

"Tibby... do you know what I want?" She looked at him expectantly.

"I want that you will always hum while you sew."

⁂

Zach rose early and left straight after he had done his morning chores. Tibby stood on the verandah and watched him sit tall in his saddle in the early dawn light. His soft kiss lingered on her lips. She jolted as she heard movement behind her and turned to see Heather staring at her brother disappearing down the track to town.

"Why hasn't he taken the cart for supplies? Where's he going? It must be important to leave in such a hurry – he hasn't had much breakfast. Will he be gone all day?"

"I believe so. He has his reasons for going to town." Her heart quickened as she saw a triumphant tilt to Heather's neck.

"Well, that gives us all day to get to know each other better. Come inside, Tabitha dear. I'm interested in the new quilt you are piecing. It seems more involved compared to the other items in the hut. You certainly have made some progress in your homely improvements."

Tibby looked at Heather and tried to smother her disgust. Even when she attempted the appearance of being agreeable, she managed to be insulting. She took a deep breath. Or perhaps she really was trying. Did she know their plans as Zach intimated? Perhaps she had made peace with the inevitable. Tibby was tired of being always on guard – they were destined to be family. If she could wish-upon-a-star one thing… it would be that family was comfortable. She turned to go inside with a prayer that somehow her relationship with Heather would be less prickly and then the picture of her life with Zach would be complete.

"Cup of tea?"

She looked at Heather suspiciously as she raised the teapot in her hand and felt a pang of guilt that she was always suspicious of her.

"Thank you, Heather, that would be nice. Good morning, Amelia. You're up early."

Amelia averted her eyes, and quickly ran to the outhouse. Heather seemed determined not to sigh or huff or be impatient this morning and handed Tibby a cup and saucer. Tibby sipped Heather's tea, a morning ritual that was a luxury she didn't grow up with and felt herself relax. She had overreacted again. Perhaps this was the turning point.

Heather sat down at the table and smiled. "You know... I think I have been a little unfair. It seems that my brother is determined to stay here, so perhaps I should give him the benefit of the doubt. It seems I hardly know him..."

Tibby responded warmly. "Oh, we would love your support in being here. I know the farm is rough and ungainly, and it isn't your cup of tea, so to speak. But you are his sister..."

"Well, it certainly does seem that he has made up his mind."

Tibby smiled. "Zach is not one to do something quickly, but once his mind is made up, he is determined alright. It seems that you know that about him well enough."

"Well..." Heather was struggling articulating what was on her mind. "I guess... I... I just want what is best for my little brother. Is that so awful?"

In all the time she had been here Tibby had never seen Heather so open. Her relief knew no bounds. Already Tibby was anticipating being able to share with Zach how her misgivings were all for nought. "Oh no! That is not awful at all. It does me good to hear that you regard Zach so well."

"You doubt that?" She looked sharp.

For a moment Tibby wondered if she had offended her yet again. "No. No. Of course not." And she drank her cuppa silently.

"Good. Because today is a special day. I have invited guests for morning tea."

"Here? Today?"

"Of course, dear. It is unreasonable to suppose that we can always be imposing on another's hospitality without reciprocating at some level. So, the early start has worked well. We can do some cooking."

"Why would you invite them without Zach being here?"

"Come dear. I didn't know my brother was planning a day-visit to town. And even if he had told me, he would never invite me along, so I have to make my own entertainment. And you know as well as I, that even if he were here, he'd be spending the day out in the paddocks, so it seems no different at all. I thought it would be fun."

With the enthusiasm of army officer, Heather supervised preparations for her social morning like a military manoeuvre. Tibby complied with her demands without resistance. Perhaps if hosting this event was successful and Heather could see how she contributed willingly, then perhaps it may go a long way towards giving Zach her support. Or at least... backing off her opposition.

The sulky arrived mid-morning. Amelia looked out the windows and whispered breathlessly, "Oh! They are here."

Tibby was finishing wiping some cups and placed them on the table.

"Good," said Heather with finality, and glided out on the rough verandah as if it was a polished marble portico. She glowed and she smiled. Tibby came and stood behind her, but when the guests stepped down from the carriage, she felt the colour drain from her face. The man in the brown double-vested jacket, stood to assist a lady in a voluminous hat with the step. She turned her head and Tibby gasped. "Alphie!" Alphie looked around and frowned slightly, and then, paused. Smiling gloriously at Heather she started gushing her willingness to be here. Another man stepped from the carriage. Only three guests. They had set the table for four.

Tibby couldn't keep her eyes off Alphie. She stood tall, her face shrouded by her ridiculously large hat. But what made her gulp was the pendant at her neck. It was Zach's cameo. That didn't make sense. She saw Heather's astonishment when Zach allowed her to wear it, yet now she didn't even comment on Alphie audaciously flaunting it in public. Of course, she must recognise it. How could she possibly agree to this?

Heather stepped forward with groomed hospitality. "Welcome my friends. Amelia, you know. Allow me to introduce... to... well... ah... a family friend. This is Tabitha... Flanders. This is Mr and Mrs Thomas Fenessy. And this is Mr Walter Bramley."

Bramley looked irked by Heather's carry on. "Call me Waldo," he said curtly, and he walked inside ahead of the rest. When they came inside, he was already sitting at the table, his chair leaned back taking in the whole room. He picked up a serviette and inspected the stitching. "Hmm," he murmured to himself.

Tibby stood to the side determined to be the polite hostess in lieu of Zach's presence. "Do you know stitching, Mr Bramley?" she asked politely.

He looked across at her. "Only on saddles," he said as if he was being hilariously witty. And then as if he had thought of something additionally clever, he added, "I break horses. That's my job... taming fillies."

Heather stepped up alongside him. "I think we will eat now. There seems to be a hold up with our remaining guest. Would you like a cup of tea, Mr Bramley?"

"Waldo."

"Tea, Mr Waldo?" complied Heather patiently.

He nodded and smirked. Amelia fussed and poured tea and removed the covers from the treats they had cooked that morning.

Mr Fenessy looked at Tibby with a brazen stare, and when he smiled there was a gap from a missing tooth. He shared a private joke with Mr Bramley, who smirked. Tibby coloured and didn't know where to look. It was all blatantly done in front of his wife. Did the man know no shame? But then, Alphie didn't seem to notice, whether on purpose or just out of a dogged refusal to acknowledge she was married to a pig, she could not be sure. She pretended to not even know Tibby, but she chatted and giggled with Amelia like life-long soulmates.

Tibby couldn't keep her eyes off Alphie. Her makeup was heavy, and there was a cut on her lip. The cameo sat on her neck like a beacon. She wished she were bold enough to rip it from her throat and escape. Mr Fenessy looked at her again and followed her eyes to his wife's necklace. "So, you like my wife's little trinket? Strangest thing..." he said with a wink, "found it... lying in the grass down by the stables. Just lying there, all covered in dirt," he said provocatively.

Tibby's face flushed and her eyes smouldered with fire. She clenched her fist behind her back in restraint. How dare Heather invite these ignorant, disgusting people into their home! How she wished Zach would come riding in from town. He would send them on their way.

Waldo's smirk became broader and spoke to Tibby directly. "You know... I wasn't too fussed about this at first, but it looks like this could be okay."

"I'm pleased you are amused by our little morning tea," Tibby said tersely. Really what was the point? "I will go and check on water for more tea," and she walked out the back and jabbed the fire over which the kettle hung.

She could hear them talking with Heather quite openly, as if they didn't understand that the little hut was neither soundproof nor large enough to muffle conversation. "She doesn't know does she? And you told me she was on board." Waldo didn't sound angry by whatever misunderstanding he referred to. That man gave her the creeps.

"Mr and Mrs Fennessy have come to an agreement with me."

"Well, well. You're a conniving little minx. I wonder what you get out of this?" At that Tibby smiled. Finally, someone saw through Heather's fine makeup and superficial manners.

"It is simple Mr Bramley... I get my way."

"Normally I don't go lightly with being taken for a fool. But in this case, I'm inclined to be amused by your... morning tea... like she said."

"Amused? I was expecting a more lasting commitment." Heather sounded high and mighty as always.

"I'll do it."

"Of course, you will. You like a challenge. And the financial sweetener is not too hard to swallow either."

When Tibby came inside, they stopped talking and Waldo said he would have fresh tea. He scoffed down some bran cake and grunted impatiently about the hold up from the other guy not showing. Mr Fenessy went out to the cart and returned with a couple of bottles of wine. He poured himself and Waldo a generous glass and they tucked into more cakes, scoffing like ten-year-old boys home from boarding school. They had another glass. And another.

Amelia surveyed the decimated table and wondered uneasily how they would cater for the additional guest. She insisted on making up a plate of the few remaining items. Alphie tried to soothe Amelia's anxiety by saying he was probably not coming for the food anyway. This catapulted Amelia's distress, and she declared it was unfair that their guests could be so unhappy with the catering when they had tried so hard to please. Alphie pointed to the crumbs on the plates as evidence that no one was unhappy with the cooking. Still, Amelia needed to explain in detail every recipe and how she had felt they had turned out reasonably well given the kitchen they had to work with. Tibby stepped back and surveyed the scene with disgust. Heather came and stood beside her.

"I hope it meets every expectation," said Tibby, trying to hold her manners in check. For Heather who was so set on appearances, it seemed ridiculous that she could consider that she had hosted a pleasant occasion.

"You do well to take it all in."

"Hump!" But there was an ungainly pause and Tibby glanced at her sickened. "Why? What do you mean?"

"Nothing. But soon... soon you will understand."

"Understand what?" The same sickening fear she had experienced down by the billabong seemed to come up to strangle her. "What are you meaning, Heather?"

"Nothing dear. You worry excessively. Our morning tea looks like it will be a raging success."

"I'm glad you think so."

"Oh, I will." And she smiled serenely and walked back and sat down and listened to Amelia's details of the pan scones recipe as if they were dazzling petit-fours.

Tibby turned to gather up some plates. She wondered how Heather's sarcasm could still cut her to the bone. She knew what she was like. When Tibby tried to use her most poisoned barb it would float past feebly, and Heather always remained unperturbed. It was like she was resistant to insult. Tibby didn't want to take on Zach's insistence that certain people were incapable of bettering themselves. She really wanted to believe that change for good was always possible. As she started washing the dishes, she had to seriously consider that perhaps some things were beyond hope. Some people. Finally, Heather picked up a remaining cup and poured elegantly from the teapot. She brought it over to Tibby and said to her, "Come inside and sit. You have been on your feet all morning. Just sit for a moment. The dishes can wait. You have been such a help."

Tibby shook her head. The woman was exhausting with her pendulum swings of snide taunts and attempts at being companionable. She took the cup of tea and sat down away from the others. Still, she'd take Heather attempts at being chummy anytime. It was just easier.

She sipped tea, and relaxed. She checked inside the cup as it tasted odd, but it seemed clean enough. Her head started to feel lighter. The weight of the morning seemed to float away. The room seemed brighter, more open; the faces around the table seemed to fade out of focus and she wanted to bask in her other reality... the reality that while they were sitting sipping strange-flavoured tea, her Zach was riding to town to secure her hand. She was loved with a strength this weak lot of individuals would never appreciate. She was loved and that was a treasure much weightier than cleverly cooked pan scones. How could they ever think this was important? They were shallow, irritating, sickening, arrogant. Waldo the creep was right. Conniving: all of them.

Her cup became very heavy, and it rattled in the saucer. She put it down on the table before her and it fell right through the table-top and smashed on the floor into a million shards. Tibby stared at the fragments in disbelief. How could something be so heavy that a table could not hold it? She looked fascinated at the pieces of china at her feet and tried to jigsaw them back together in her mind. If she concentrated really hard, she was sure she could fix it.

Someone walked through the door. "Zach...?" She didn't expect him home until later, so did that mean everything went well? Or did something go wrong? She jolted when Heather came and stood her to her feet.

"This is Father Crowley..."

That struck Tibby as extremely funny. Crowley was dressed in black. His robes made him look like a crow. She giggled. Crowley. Crow. How fitting.

Waldo came and stood beside him. Creepy Waldo and the crow. They made an uncanny pair. The crow started to caw, in a strange grating voice that sent chills up and down her spine. She noticed those chills in a kind of detached curious way. It felt like someone had a broom handle and was running it up and down her back. The crow went on and on. Creepy Waldo said something.

The crow was looking at her. Someone jabbed her ribs and she let out a yelp. They were pulling at her then. Pushing her to write something. Pulling at her to carry her bag that sat on her freshly made bed. Pushing her into the cart. She didn't want to get in the cart. Zach was coming home. She needed to stay to find out when Zach was going to marry her.

18.

Tibby's head started to thump in rhythm to the sway of the cart where she had slumped exhausted. To start with she was hardly aware of it... but she became conscious of it as if someone was poking hot irons through her temples jabbing her awake. She didn't want to wake. Her limbs were weighted with lead. She wanted to stay asleep: oblivious to the pain in her head; cushioned in a world where Heather's bullying could no longer touch her.

Another cart ride echoed around her body where the pain searing through her made everything fuzzy. Is that why she felt so disconnected to her body now? A sense of foreboding constricted her in a terrifying sheath. And she felt herself starting to spin, starting to scream silent screams. She tried to breathe, tried to focus, tried to see where she was, but nothing made sense. Zach should have been here. He said was going to marry her. Did he lie? Did he send them? Did he go away so they could come?

Zach leapt off his horse and pounded through the hut calling out. He got to the cookhouse in three strides. He came back inside and looked at Heather sitting calmly at the table reading a book. "Where is she?"

"Who, my dear?"

"Don't give me your condescending guff. What have you done?"

"You seem so certain that your kitchen maid is not here. She may be out doing chores since you left so early."

Zach moved quickly and grabbed Heather's lace collar, tearing its fine threads under his grip. "What did you do? Tell me!"

A look of surprise, shock, respect, and fear, flickered through her eyes in a sequence of seconds. "Zachary you are spoiling my dress. I..."

"What have you done? Where is she?" He's tone matched his ice-cold eyes.

"She's..." She couldn't say it.

"Amelia!" She appeared at his summons; timid with down turned eyes. "Where is Tabitha?"

"Amelia..." cautioned Heather quietly.

"Sir... she, ahh... left after... the priest... to Mr..." She started to cry.

Zach glared hard at Heather, and she unfolded a copy of a certificate and pushed it onto the table in silence. He stared at and realised what had happened. Something dangerous smouldered in his eyes. "When I get back you will be packed and gone."

"Zachary! You can't do anything. It is legally done. It is over. We will just have to make a different..."

"Get out! Get out!!!"

He jumped on his horse and pounded across the culvert to Bates' place. Where else would Heather have found a willing groom at such short notice? She'd been planning this while he was living in his blissful state of naivety believing that his own blood could not... would not be so vile! Tibby had been right to be scared. She knew the potential of her evil.

He didn't go up to the big house but stopped at the workers' village. He knocked at a low-set shack in the cluster of scrappy shanties. A burly man opened the door; his tattoos gave his Maori face a fierce look. He stooped under the doorframe as he stood there, and then he wordlessly stepped aside to let Zach in.

Ol' Hilda was sitting in a low-slung chair sewing by the light from an open shutter. She looked up nonplussed. "Guess you heard," she said as she tied off a stitch.

"Tell me what you know."

"They passed by a while back. She looked dazed."

"Was she hurt? Who was it? Who was with her?"

Hilda pursed her fleshy lips and went back to her sewing. Zach appealed to the man. "Tacko... help me out here mate."

"They'll kill ya, you know. Is she worth it?"

The rage in his head exploded. He flung out and slogged him. Tacko shook him off and tackled him like a runaway steer, pinning him to the dirt floor of their hut, while he thrashed. Eventually Zach stilled. Old Hilda got up and poured a pannikin of home-brew. Tacko held him by the collar at arm's length while Hilda handed him the mug. He took a swig, allowing it to fuel the fire in his head.

"You gotta get a grip," offered Tacko. "You have to be smart about this. You can't go up there or you'll be dead, and the girl with you. This ain't the first time they be treat'n and trading girls like horseflesh."

Hilda grunted. "Horses get better..."

Zach's body tensed and coiled, and Hilda poured him another mug of brew.

For ten days he brawled and drank himself numb, to silence the screaming in his head, while Tacko and Hilda patiently bore his rage and his outbursts and poured him drinks, sacrificing their precious home-brew in service of a friend.

Tibby woke up in a daze. She started upright as she realised that she was in an unfamiliar place. She looked over and saw The Creep sleeping beside her. The room started swirling. Her breathing came fast. She started screaming inside her head again. Waldo's eyes flew open, and he jumped out of bed in horror. "What's wrong with you woman! Shut up!"

Even if she had wanted to, she couldn't. She scrambled out of the bed and huddled in the corner and screamed louder when he came close.

"You don't get it, do you? You're married to me. You're my wife. Pull yourself together!" He looked at her in disgust. "I ain't come across no filly yet that was wild enough I couldn't tame." Still, that was for later. Just now he had overslept; he had a headache from the celebratory wine and had to go to work. He shackled her on a long rope and left the house with crass promises of honeymoon favours and marital taming.

The morning settled in, and the huts around them stilled as the workers dissipated to their various jobs. Tibby sat huddled in the corner, the rope around her ankle like a dog. She tried to regulate her breathing. She had heard his announcement. She was married. To him. She shuddered and slowed her breathing again. That's what the afternoon tea with Waldo the Creep was about. She pieced together the haze of memories. Heather had finally worked out a way to get rid of her. She looked at her left hand and there was a thin cheap ring on her finger. She pulled it off and threw it at the fireplace. Zach had declared his love. Straight out. No riddles.

She threaded the rope through the hut and locked herself in the out-house. She had to settle. She had to make a plan. Zach might be able do something about this from his side, but he may not. If she ran, they may take retribution on Zach for taking what was legally someone's property. She had to find a way to convince Waldo the Creep that his life was better without her. He had to send her back. She remembered the Bible story of David, scratching at the door and dribbling down his beard like a madman so that his enemies decided he was more of a liability than an asset.

She knew it would rile him. She knew it would cost her a beating or more. But he was going to want to get rid of her. She went back inside and cooked herself some breakfast. She was going to need to be as healthy and strong as she could for this. She pulled out Zach's bible that had been packed in her bag and read the story again and prayed for strength. She left her things packed and stashed them outside. By the time he came home she was sitting calmly by the table with a bedsheet as a tablecloth, the kerosene lantern lit and she was sewing. Waldo came through the door and his face relaxed as he saw her sitting there. She had certainly come to the party easier than he had imagined. She was a picture of domestic harmony. She looked up and smiled inanely. "I found my sewing," she said in a monotone voice. "I do sewing."

He frowned then. This was not the feisty filly that had seen at the morning tea. This was not the panic stricken wild-woman he left this morning huddled in the corner. This was something else altogether.

"Where's dinner?"

She shrugged. "I do sewing," she said.

"Well, you're going to have to cook too."

"I can sew."

"But that's not all wives do. They cook. They clean. Then they sew."

"Yes! I sew. See – I found buttons missing. I sew." And she lifted up the shirt that she had on her lap and displayed the buttons that she had replaced. They were big and round and looked very out of place.

He stared at it in disbelief. "Where did you get those buttons?"

"I found them. I sew."

He went to the nail where his jacket hung in the corner. "You idiot! You've destroyed my best coat!" He stared at the front of his coat that had three very large holes cut neatly around the buttons down the front.

"Oh. Don't worry... I'll mend it. I sew."

He reached out to hit her and she cowered in shock. He paused as if something restrained him, then he hit her across the face anyway. "Now get up and fix me dinner!"

She simpered rubbing the red welt from his hand on her cheek. "Yes sir. I thought you liked me to sew. You like my stitching."

"Get up and get me dinner!"

She jumped to her feet, picking up her sewing kit with her. Dragging the rope, she ran out to the kitchen. She had wound the rope around the leg of the chair and sewn the tablecloth to the hem of her dress, and it pulled everything off the table, the kerosene lamp crashed to the floor and the blue flames quickly licking up the spilt fuel trailing after her. She could hear him screeching profanities as he ran to put out the fire. She calmly picked up a clever and hacked the rope from her ankle and with a knife, sliced the tablecloth from her skirt and walked outside the burning hut. She sat down beside some cold left-over stew she found in a pot and watched the world erupting around her as workers activated in a manic effort to put out the fire. They couldn't. The hut burnt to the ground, but they managed to save the huts around it from catching.

Waldo evicted one of the single workers to the stables and took over his hut. He sat down to eat. "Damn you woman! You've burnt my things... my best saddle." Tibby brought in a plate of the leftover stew she found in the hearth and put it on the table as if she was unaware of the chaos and scorched war zone that they had just encountered. He picked up his spoon and gagged. Then he tossed it away, splashing stew all over the table, chair, and floor. "This is not fit for a dog! Get me something to eat!" Tibby went and loudly rummaged through the unfamiliar panty hutch and found some dry bread and dripping. She cut a slab, and he took it swearing impatiently and demanding that she clean up the mess while he went to bed.

Tibby pouted, "I do sewing. I do sewing."

"Shut up woman!" he yelled, "Clean it up!" and rolled over covering his ears with a pillow while Tibby continued murmuring, occasionally dropping, or clanging the pot. If the price of another night reprieve was cleaning up a little stew, it was certainly worth it. And as she wiped away stew in the light of a lone candle, she set herself the creative task of thinking up more disruption.

Hilda gave Tacko the nod, her lips firm and her eyes determined. Tacko lifted Zach up like a kitten by the scruff of the neck and took him down to the creek. They stripped him to his drawers and threw him in the water. He spluttered and swore and swayed as he stood up. Hilda threw him some laundry soap and a threadbare towel, and he looked at them stupidly. They both waded into the water determined to wash him like a woolly wether being presented for shearing. They handed him a razor and fragment of mirror and he shook as he shaved the scruff off his chin, cutting his cheek. Hilda presented him with a clean set of clothes that hung on his lean frame like a sack. And then she gave him a concoction to drink to ease the thumping in his head.

He sat on an upturned wooden bucket outside their hut with a tin mug of bushman's coffee in his hand that tasted like burnt toast scrapings diluted with muddy water. He said nothing for a long time. Tacko refilled his mug again and said, "So what ya going to do Mate?"

"Dunno. What's the point? Doesn't matter what I do. Someone with more brains, or more bread, or more brawn, takes what they want anyhow."

"Nothing wrong with your smarts. You've survived on your own. Of course, it figures you're going to be a target. You're an independent."

"Huh." The way Tacko said it, his self-appointed perseverance was an admirable virtue. He didn't see it that way. He was betrayed. Never in his wildest imagination could he have conceived his sister would be that malicious. He sat there. His rage boiling like the water that made his coffee. He didn't have the foresight to protect Tibby. He never saw this coming. Even when he got to town and was told Father Crowley was out doing pastoral visitation and would be back soon, he had waited. If he hadn't waited...

He had passed the priest on his way back home, and he introduced himself. When Zach introduced himself and said he had waited in town for an appointment, suddenly the priest wouldn't talk to him, or even look at him. He became invisible. The priest tipped his hat and just continued on his way. Zach chased him down and demanded an audience. Finally, Crowley took notice. It wasn't until the priest called him *'fornicating filth that would burn in hell if he pursued the matter'*, that Zach realised something was wrong. He sat on his horse stunned that such venom would come from a man of the cloth. He had gone his way when Zach realised, he hadn't said exactly what he had wanted to discuss with him. He considered that perhaps the priest somehow knew Tibby's traumatic history, or heard she was staying at Dellaweir without being married. But even then, he never imagined this.

He wouldn't allow himself to think about what was happening to her. The pain and the injury he witnessed when she was dumped at his gate... that would be hers... again. Only this time he was not there to pick up the pieces. Reports came back from the house staff. They had heard screaming. Waldo was allocated a hut in the privileged sector closer to the stables where the overseers and managers lived. That hut had burnt down. Then they took another place. Yet *privilege* at the Bates spread was still squalor, unless you lived at the homestead. Zach no longer felt any apology for his own offer: what he offered was better than that. He offered his love.

He laid down that night at Ol' Hilda's, on the makeshift swag made from hessian bags and a couple of thin blankets. He looked at the stars through the cracks between the slab timbered wall of Tacko and Hilda's hut, and by the time those stars faded, and the sky became lighter, he had determined something. It had nothing to do with accepting the inevitable; or getting on with life; or making a different plan, as Heather had suggested.

They sat on their upturned buckets, mugs of coffee in hand, and Hilda bought out a slab of dry bread that they used to chase some wallaby stew around his plate. When he was done, he looked over to Tacko.

"I'm going home. Like you said: I gotta be smart about this. I am going to get her back. I'm just not good at their game. That's what I gotta learn: how to play their bloody-minded game. I'm going to study the rules. And I am going to win."

Tacko nodded. He said nothing. He stood up and went and collected Zach's horse.

As he mounted, Zach looked at Ol' Hilda. "You get a message to her. Let her know I'm coming. I'm not giving up and she is not to either. Tell her to do whatever she has to do, to survive... for me. And for her to be ready."

19

Zach dismounted and sighed as he tethered his horse. This looked very different from what he had imagined he would be doing over a week ago. He froze at the door as he heard Heather reproaching Amelia inside. He took a deep breath. He opened the door and Heather looked up from where she was sitting at the table with a teacup in her hand. "Well good morning," she said breezily. Her smile seemed to indicate that if she were mild enough, all would be forgiven. "It has been a while. Where have you been?" she said as she sat her teacup back in its saucer.

Zach didn't pause. "I told you to leave. And yet you are still here. Get your things. I'm taking you to town. Now."

"Zach! I can't possibly go to town. Where would I stay?"

"You've had plenty of time to sort it out. Not my problem if you haven't."

"But I am your sister! You have responsibilities toward me."

"Last week blood ties meant nothing to you."

"But it does. I'll prove it. I have Mother's cameo locket. See? It was part of..."

"You did what?"

She pulled it out and dangled it from her hand. "I only did it to save you fr..."

He grabbed it and cut her off. "Get your things or I will take you without them! Whatever you leave, I will burn. I'm hitching the cart." He walked out, immune to her screeching. He harnessed the horse and could hear Heather demanding Amelia to quickly get their things sorted. He shook his head. What happened to her? He only had contempt for Heather, but he felt very sorry for Amelia. Society was not an equitable trade for dignity. How dearly Amelia paid for aligning herself so completely with someone disinterested in any one's well-being other than her own. How dearly *he* paid.

He waited by the cart. He knew they were stalling. When Heather came out, she looked entirely peeved, and Zach noticed with another sigh he didn't care. He was done. Her dissatisfaction or approval was equally meaningless. "Better load your things," is all he said. But, as he watched Heather berate Amelia over her efforts, it got the better of him and he loaded their trunks. When Heather insisted the chest that stood under the window be brought out, Zach stepped in.

"That trunk stays. Now get on or I will physically hog-tie you to the running board."

Heather stopped short. This was a Zachary she did not know. She scrambled up onto the hard seat; tears of humiliation stinging her eyes; another chorus of complaint, about all the ill treatment, hardship, and inconvenience began. Zach said nothing but flicked the reigns and moved out.

Heather's tone quickly changed from petulant protest, to accusation, and then threats, and finally a pronouncement that she held no regret for what she had done, as it was all executed in the best interests of protecting their family name. He sat expressionless and drove on. The idea of the woman beside him was repulsive. He silently restrained the smouldering rage that was seething through every pore in his body. If he got to town without strangling her, that would be the best Christian service he could manage just now.

When they arrived into town, he pulled over beside the hotel and wordlessly unloaded the trunks and cases to the kerb. He waited until they scrambled down, mutely flicked the reigns again and turned the cart towards home without looking back. He unhitched the cart and tended the animals, silently without his usual mumbled commentary of husbandry concern.

When he came inside, he went straight to the bedroom. He pulled off the patch-worked throw and tossed it to the side. The linen and mattress was flung in the corner. Then he went out to the wood-pile and brought in the axe. Then he let his rage take vent. He smashed every inch of it. He dragged the mattress and linen outside and threw the splintered timber on top and burnt the lot. That woman had slept on this and defiled it. He regretted that he had been too shy to tell Tibby he had always intended this would be their marriage bed. There was no way in perdition he was going to sleep in a bed with his wife, when that woman had lounged in that very same place plotting her self-righteous, malevolent treachery. He would make another: one reserved exclusively for Tibby as his wife, one that had bold, blatant love in the carpentry.

Uncle Cedric once told Zachary that his father's life at sea was not his first choice but that he had wanted to be a barrister. His ambition for improvement captivated him, so he married into a family of privilege. Ced maintained however, that once his social position was locked in, so were the demands needed to sustain it. The sea became his only realistic option, as the merchant navy afforded better money than the study of law would ever deliver. When Zach was about twelve, he was told his father had been struck with illness while he was overseas and never recovered. That was when Cedric also handed Zach a letter in which his father urged him to do the book learning needed to be a professional man – a lecturer, or a doctor, or a magistrate. Ced had thumped him on his back, thus fulfilling his obligation to his brother. Zach had folded away the letter and rode out to muster cattle. Zach's relationship with his father had been remote, even when he was home between trips. As he got older, Zach thought it was ridiculous to suppose he would make a life decision based on a message his father couldn't even deliver in person. It was hardly an option to follow some vicarious career path to satisfy a dead man's perceived failure, even if that man was his father.

All in all, Uncle Ced had skirted around the idea of book-learning to make it sound just like a different version of Aunt Peony's pretension. It was the Logan curse: to desire to be more in the eyes of society and they ended up selling their souls for the privilege. His other uncles were the same. Well, not Ced, and not him. Farming was enough. Well, it had been until now.

He never thought farming would lead him down a road of book-learning, but now he had no choice. Again, he was backed into a corner and his time had come. Damnation. His father had been right: learning did have its uses. He determined that if Tibby was to get out of this prison alive, he needed to know the rules and make every action watertight.

He got up and cleared the table of the things that were there and piled them on the sideboard. Until Tibby came home, he wouldn't need these comfortable things about him. He walked over to the trunk that stood under the shuttered window. He knelt down and opened the lid. A shot of musty air wafted from the books inside and made him cough. There were other things as well: maps, an old-fashioned ivory writing set with an inkpot, some bookends decorated with travel globes and a case with a pair of eyeglasses. These things had belonged to his father.

He opened a book and looked at the pages in frustration. Everything seemed grey. He pushed the table over to the window and opened the shutter. He set the lamp on the table and turned it up, but the words seemed shrouded in a haze. It occurred to him then, to try the eyeglasses. He cleaned the lenses carefully and tried them on tentatively. He looked at the page and the words snapped into focus. He took them off and the words retreated. He put them on again and the print became clear. It amazed him. He opened another book and stared at the pages before him. Words jumped from the page in clarity. He grabbed a newspaper from the pile from town and started searching the classified section. Right now, his mission was specific. He needed help and he needed to find where to get it.

He knew his reading was rudimentary at best, but he had no doubt that this was something he could improve with practice. Perhaps a lot of practice. He smiled as he thought of Tibby's lists. He might make a list. In fact, that would give him something to write. The changes he needed to make now rotated around getting the book-learning he needed, in the same the way that his day revolved around the sun rising in the east and setting over the hills in the west.

Zach was dressed in his suit, and he had his eyeglasses in his pocket. He went inside and sat in the waiting area. The room was cluttered and untidy. He saw a mouse scuttle through the open door to an office that was also a chaotic pile of books and files and loose papers. He didn't really know how to get the information he needed.

A man named Bailey ushered him into the office and moved some books off the seat opposite his desk. He shuffled some papers between the piles in front of him and moved away some newspapers. Bailey had been pouring over bits of paper tabulated with names and numbers. He put it aside distractedly, and asked with a very bored yawn, what he could do to help.

Zach cleared his throat. He thought if he presented as a thwarted lover there was little chance that he would even get a hearing. It might be more convincing if he played the role of the wronged spouse. Unfortunately, he was a terrible actor. "I want information about filing for divorce."

The man glanced up and saw Zach squirm. He wasn't at all interested in his personal tragedy. "Wanting one is common. Getting one isn't. How long you been married?"

"Not long."

"Well, you have to wait at least a couple of years... most judges expect five."

"Still want the information."

"There isn't a judge in the British Empire who will just give you a divorce. Even if you can prove you were wronged, and you couldn't hold your family together, it might not hold up. Just because your woman is a whore and makes your life hell, doesn't make it sure."

"So, there's no hope of it going through, even though it's wrong from beginning to end?"

"It happens; just not often. Could go for an annulment – and let the church handle it; that isn't much simpler, just more likely. As they say, *marriage is a God ordained institution that the state and church must protect.*" He certainly didn't look convinced of the sanctity of that divine commission.

"Are you a learned man, Mr Bailey?"

"Yeah. Done my time. Why?"

"You don't sound particularly so, that's all. I was expecting more."

"Huh. I don't get paid for elocution. I get paid on facts, interpretation, and advice."

"I heard there were particular sectors of our community that had cut you off. That's why I came here."

Bailey looked at him. He seemed mildly less disinterested than when he first sat down, and he cleared his throat. He noticed the man hadn't asked to verify that; it was just an observation. "Most people come to me because I'm their last desperate alternative," he said with candid honesty. A few clients considered that he was a preferred option to the only other legal counsel in town: Crosby and Moore.

"Well, if desperate is the criteria, then I probably fit. I also want some information... a reference really."

"I've got some connections. Most of them are expensive."

"I want someone to tutor me law."

The man stared at him over his desk and then laughed outright. "I'll be damned. You're the oddest kettle of fish I ever seen. A tutor!"

Zach didn't move and he didn't smile. The man settled down, shook his head, and swore. "If I'd be a betting man... and I am... I'd be thinking you don't want the divorce at all. She does? Yeah. I thought so. She's got you over a barrel. You need to lift your game."

"Nearly. She was forced to marry against her will. What I need, is to get her back."

"Oh. Personal."

"I would have thought any divorce was personal."

"Maybe. Most are about hate."

"Oh, I have a fair quota of hate," admitted Zach without hesitation.

He shrugged. "Well, this is a change on the usual scenario, and since I spend a great deal of time being bored, that is something. Who's the groom?"

"Does it make any difference?"

"I need details if I'm going to take the case."

"So, you'll do it? What about the tutoring?"

"I'll tell you what. We'll come to an agreement. I'll take your case, and your tutoring. I've got no clerk, and there's a few things I never get around to doing, which I probably should. If you do whatever I need: bookwork, filing, rat extermination, washing up... you can work off your account. You do look... versatile."

Zach considered him. Being versatile just now was inconvenient for sure; but if he was going to learn the rules he just had to start. "Okay. Done."

"Alright then. Let's get the details. The aggrieved? The bride? Address? The respondent? That's the other person. When was the alleged wedding? Who officiated?" His flow of questions dried up. He stared at him. "I'm guessing this was one of Bates' men since you haven't reported it as a kidnapping to the constable."

Zach shrugged. He placed the certificate of marriage on a pile of papers between them. "I didn't think kidnapping would stick. That, and yes, he is a Bates' man."

Bailey talked for a while about Collusion Clauses, something about collaborating with the aggrieved to get the story weighted in their favour. None of which made any sense to Zach at all. In the end Bailey just said, "Go for the annulment. We'll file it with the bishop and leave Crowley out of it since he's so embedded in Bates' sheets he looks like the proverbial bedbug. That's your best bet." It seemed to Zach that Maurice Bailey judged matters of law according to gambling "odds". Perhaps that was all it was.

❧

Zach returned to the office Thursday to begin his tutoring. The first thing that Bailey did when he turned up was hand him a list of chores. Zach grimaced. "Do this. Then I'll give you some time with the books."

"Today? That's a long list."

"Then you'd better get busy, if you're going to finish early enough."

That first day Zach did nothing other than sort the front reception room. He scrubbed the floors and cleared the newspapers and put up a shelf. He mended a chair and the rickety low table. At the end of the day, he was surprised how much Tibby was in this room. He crossed off the first three items on the list and came to Bailey.

He folded his newspaper to the side and looked at the list. "You didn't get far."

"You didn't expect me to."

"I expected you to get bored and leave." Yes, he had anticipated Logan would lose interest and abandon this idea.

"Then you don't know me."

"Huh." So now what? He couldn't just teach this guy things in an afternoon that had taken him years to learn. "Okay then. Umm... Well then, the best thing you can do for yourself is become a reader. The principles of Law are found in books. So, learn to read fast and well."

"I don't have too many books at home."

Bailey swept his eyes over the dust, cobwebs and ridiculously large mountains of books piled around his few overburdened bookcases in the room. He went over to a stack in the corner. "Always meant to install shelves around the walls. Might get to that now." He picked up a volume. "When you find your way around the books, you will have access to what you need. No amount of tutoring can do that for you. When you've read this, we can talk more about your tuition then." Baily grinned and handed Zach a sheet outlining the hours of work against professional services rendered. He was pretty sure he wouldn't have to discuss this again – ever. Bailey had two loves. Horse-racing and books. It figured it was time to indulge his love of books. They had been neglected too long.

Zach looked at the clock on Bailey's cluttered mantle. Five minutes. That was the sum of his tutoring for today. He took the book silently and returned home. The eyeglasses explained a lot to him. He knew how to read, but it had always seemed a laborious bother to understand the blur on the page. He learnt by memorising the black board in the little country school that Uncle Cedric had sent him to. And when it came to close work... reading and writing, it felt like he was feeling his way in the dark. After he completed his chores, he pulled out the writing set and sat it on the table. He fumbled through setting the nib and loading the ink and then wrote his name. His signature he could do blind. He got up and rummaged through the trunk and pulled out all the books. He found a large volume, a dictionary. He started to compile his list, carefully tracing the letters as he remembered them, checking them against the letters in the book. Then he copied some texts from the bible, reading them out loud. The words infused life into his soul. He needed this.

Every so often he would get up from reading the volume Bailey had given him and take a break to work on some chores. He could hardly make a declaration for Tibby to be ready, if he was not prepared himself. He needed to organise his time in a regimented routine so he could finish Tibby's new kitchen; he needed a bed; he needed... her.

He took the book with him and started, breaking the monotony of reading with other jobs around the farm. Bailey declared the volume would open up the world of Law to him. But as he was reading – he felt frustrated and fobbed off. There was not one piece of legislation, no court records, no judge rulings. It was a laborious account of English maritime history. He threw it aside for three days, the irony that the book celebrated his father's world fuelling his frantic construction of formwork for the mudbrick moulds. Then he started filling them with slurry from the edge of the lagoon. Then he sheepishly returned to reading the book because he realised if he was to get another five minutes out of Mr Bailey, reading this text was the price he had to pay.

20.

The locals had never seen this particular waterhole less than half empty, but this drought was shrinking it to a puddle. Fast. The receding water level was like a tide going out. However, it gave him unfettered access to copious amounts of clay-saturated mud: perfect for brick making. He developed a routine of making slurry, with added manure for binding, filled up his moulds quickly, and he slapped them with the back of a paddle to work out the bubbles. It was accomplished with relative ease, but there was no satisfaction in it. He scrubbed the mud and slurry off his work clothes and washed in the remaining stagnating waterholes at the end of the day. He felt a pang of despair, picturing Tibby splashing and floating during her swimming lessons, gaining rudimentary confidence in the water. How different this would have been; should have been. When he knocked the formwork away, the rows of bricks looked like a child's city made out of blocks. Streets and laneways appeared along the side of the lagoon as he stood them on their end to dry.

He returned to Mr Bailey's two weeks later. Zach walked in and was greeted with raised eyebrows. "You've still got hours to pay for my services."

"I know. You asked me to read the book," said Zach as he placed it on his table.

"I wanted you to read it cover to cover."

"I did."

"What was it about then?"

148

Zach shrugged. "English imperialism. Didn't really know what that even meant, but I looked it up. Boring as counting sheep in my mind. Didn't have anything to do with law."

"Our Queen is English, our law, our judges and governors are English; our military is English. We're not ever going to get away from that. If we lived somewhere else, we'd be reading Spanish history in Spanish... or French history in French. Getting a handle on how it has worked for the Mother Country over the years is a proper place to start."

Zach grunted. "Huh. Thought it was a test to see if I could stick it out."

"Doesn't matter to me one iota whether you stick it out or not." He handed Zach his list of chores with a few more added to the bottom. Zach went to work pulling books off shelves in the office along one wall. He drew up a plan of wall-to-wall shelving and went over to the sawmill to order supplies. He continued clearing out the space, measuring and marking out well past lunchtime. At four o'clock he stopped and went to Maurice.

Bailey looked up from his desk where he had been calculating something. "I want you to come in more regular."

"I got a farm to run."

"I thought you had an annulment to file."

"I do... and tutoring."

"Okay. Read the book again."

"That's my next tutoring lesson?"

"I think it will take you longer this time. You said yourself you just read it to prove you can stick it out. Well points for you, you've proven that. Now do it for the information the book provides."

Zach swore and took the volume with him. Was he being duped? Was he just a cheap clerk and housekeeper? As he said, there was no skin off Baily's nose whether he stuck it out or not. Still, he made a valid point: information. When he tried to recall what he had read, nothing came to mind: just meaningless words, dates, and confusing terms. He swore again and decided if he didn't get this done, he'd be reading it again, and again. That didn't seem sensible use of his time.

With his wardrobe burnt, Waldo collected some items of clothing from round about. Tibby neatly mended holes in his coat. She used fabric from a town shirt to do it. She mended that shirt from one of his work flannels. She mended his work shirt with material from the bed sheet. Hilda brought in some discarded dresses and linen from the homestead and Tibby made clothes for the children on the station; some pinafores and aprons for the women. But for every proper garment she made for the station community, she did something odd to Waldo's. She cut out dresses from the middle of the bedsheets still made on the bed. She sewed up the bottoms of the legs of Waldo's work trousers. She did the same with some of his shirts, sewing the ends of cuffs together. When he ripped the sleeves off, she sewed them back on, upside down.

Each day Waldo came home to see her mending by whatever light was available, or even sitting in the dark. She made herself not bathe and smeared herself with filth. She never said anything to him except, "I sew." She ate well while he was out but refused to prepare his meals. When he went ballistic over the laundry, she drenched everything in the house she could lay her hands on without actually cleaning it and hung it up all over the hut, ensuring it was dripping over the bed. The next day he came back with Old Hilda. "Look at her, will you? The woman's a nutter."

Hilda stood at the door while Tibby sewed at the table. "She looks okay to me. She's sewing."

"But that's all she does. She's crazy."

"When you made this arrangement, what did they tell you?"

"That there was a pretty little woman who was ... damn... that Logan woman said she was good at sewing."

"Perhaps she didn't lie. She seems to be good at sewing."

"But that's not a wife. She don't cook. She don't wash anything... even herself. She burnt the hut down. This morning I woke up and she were sewing me to the sheets! She's started muttering about sewing my mouth together."

"I've heard of... cases..." Hilda turned away and seemed reluctant to say anything further.

"What? Damn, Ol' Hilda, you tell me."

"Well, heard that in cases like this they get more and more fixated. It's because they're not... well... not where they're used to bein'. Nothing you can do about it... if that's what it is. But I ain't say'n that this is like that."

"It just gets worse? It can't get worse. She hasn't got a wheel loose... the whole shebang is falling apart! She's bonkers!"

"It could be they knew she was like that and wanted to get rid of her. Did you meet her beforehand? What was she like then?"

"Hell, I don't remember. I just remember her asking if I liked her stitching or something."

"Oh. You didn't... say something... like... to encourage her, did you? To make her think you were...pleased?" Ol' Hilda sounded frightened.

"Well, I dunno. I think I just said I thought it was a decent thing for a woman to do. But this ain't decent! This is god-damned cracked!"

"And the woman who introduced you..."

"She paid me a bucket load of cash..."

"Oh? Really?"

"And told me not to say." Waldo sat down with a thump. "That woman's a god-damned con!" Tibby now seemed irrelevant. Old Hilda said nothing. When he looked up, he caught a look of barefaced sympathy infused into Ol' Hilda's weathered face. "I don't need your pity, you old fool," he said.

"Well, I'll leave you to it then," and she turned to leave.

"Oi!" he called out. Ol' Hilda paused at the door. "If it is this thing... like you said. How do you fix it?"

"You don't. Just get them back to what they is used to... and see if it settles down some. Probably won't though, not when it's this far gone. But I'm guessin' that they knew that already though... if they gave you money. Had to get rid of her. Not like brides around here are so aplenty that you have to pay people to take 'em." She paused then. "But your secret's safe with me. I won't be telling any that the Logan woman conned you."

"But the marriage thing..."

"Hell, I don't know nothing about legal stuff. I reckon they might hit you up for alimony, or whatever they call it... for her ongoing care. She's going to need doctors. Maybe that's what it was about... since they ain't rolling in it over there."

"The hell they will!" He dragged Tibby to her feet. Her sewing things crashed to the floor, and she tried to scramble them all together. "You get up. I'm tak'n you back. Now." He pulled her up by her bedraggled hair, dragged her out to his horse and flung her across the saddle. She sat limp and said nothing... her heart beating. He dumped her at Logan's verandah. "Hey, Logan! Your Nutter is back. Tell that con-artist sister of yours, that you will never find me. Good luck if she thinks she is going to get any dosh out of me," he yelled. And like that, Waldo disappeared. Old Hilda told them later that he never went back to the station, and the general consensus was that he changed his name and moved on... most likely to the goldfields.

21.

Tibby sat quietly in the squatter's chair for a long time. She felt like she should cry, but there was nothing inside her except a vacant wash of blank relief. Skitter lay beside her, reminiscent of those early days when they were alone and unencumbered by Heather's interference. Tibby saw all the homely things they had made together were pushed to the side. A fear hovered in her chest that perhaps Zach had cleared out his life and wanted to go back to his uncomplicated bachelor days. She got up and walked around. Heather and Amelia's things were gone. She noticed the bedroom was empty and she saw the axe cuts hacked into the floorboards.

She went outside and drew herself a bath from the water barrels sitting in a row. She took the shears from the rack in the shed and cropped off her filthy hair. She took off her clothes and burnt them in the fireplace and then sat in the bath and scrubbed and scrubbed and scrubbed. And when she dressed in one of the calico shirts she had made for Zach, she filled a basin of water and scrubbed the floor and bench, working passed daylight into the evening using the light of a lamp.

By the time she heard him ride up she had scrubbed her way around the room and was near the back door. He paused outside the door before he stepped cautiously into the room, rifle cocked in his hand. He saw her kneeling on the floor, skin rubbed raw, hair cropped short, scrubbing brush in hand. He was beside her in a second. He desperately lifted her off the floor, holding her tight as her breathing came in rasping gasps.

Finally, it was over. She was home. She was safe.

He was home. He was safe. And he loved her still.

And then she did cry. Sobbing relief that came from deep within.

He held her as a man who found his precarious grip on the world restored and hung on for dear life. Instinctively Tibby felt her body stiffen and she pushed away. Zach noticed the fear in her eyes. He realised again that her story had more pain than love. He went to her gently and lifted her chin. "I am going to marry you, Tibby. I will. I don't want you to be afraid of me." He kissed her forehead, her prickly hair damp from her exertion of scrubbing away the contamination of memories.

She shivered under his touch and nodded. And went out to the kitchen to fix a light dinner. They ate on chairs in the dim light of the lamps, balancing plates on their laps. Zach said nothing. Words were not needed to explain his relief, or his mission to better protect his family.

The next morning, she woke with a jolt and then orientated to Zack's quiet commentary by the fire outside. She stirred and came out as he was adding damper to the fire. He turned and swallowed as he saw her in his shirt with short-cropped hair.

Tibby ran her hand through her hair self-consciously. "A bonnet might be my next sewing project," she said sheepishly. She poured their drinks and told of her relief when Ol' Hilda came with his message. Together they had stitched up a plan to escape the net that had been cast and willingly Ol' Hilda collaborated her insanity. She had systematically infiltrated every household with the crazy-woman story; a word here, a dropped comment there. Stories filtered back to Waldo so that everyone he knew had a story about their loony Great Aunt Fanny and wild cousin Beecher.

Zach shook his head in admiration. He had to ask. "Did he hurt you badly?"

She showed him her bruises. "I got a beating most days. If he was not working hard, he was drinking hard. In a way it was a kind of protection I didn't expect, because in the end he hardly came back. Mostly he slept at the stables with another girl."

She stood up and went on with her chores; she fed Skitter and the chooks, cut some wood for the fire and got things ready to cook a proper dinner. She uncovered the sewing machine, and did what she could, but she had lost her hand sewing kit. It was her go-to thing. But it had also been her 'crazy thing', and in a way, it was a relief at the moment to do other things that were normal.

Tibby walked over to the dining table jammed up against the wall, arranged with the lamp and inkwell by the window. She picked up the volume, *A Study of English Imperial History*, and noticed the notes that were tucked inside. She saw a sheet of paper with his name practised down the page. She found her journal... wrapped in a runner that she had embroidered for the sideboard, with a list of things to do. Tibby read the scrawled writing with a frown. Her notion that Zach could not read or write was obviously misplaced. She had assumed he had hired a scribe to write the letter to his sister. Lots of people did that. Her frown deepened. This was not a Zach she was familiar with. This did not seem like the same man who asked her to read his bills for him.

Zach came in and looked at her soberly as she stood by the table scattered with books. "Tibby, do you want to go somewhere else? If staying here is too much we'll leave," he said.

"Zach – you've put your life blood into this farm. You built it all from scratch. You know we can't leave."

"There is nothing to say we have to stay."

"No. No. You can't."

"Well, yes, we can. If we want to." He came over and pulled out the chair and sat down. He told her about his father's eyeglasses and his books and the rather frustrating reading assignments set by Maurice Bailey. "I need to fight in a way that is more... informed. I need to get some learning."

"But what about Dellaweir? You love farming."

"Not giving up on it. It's just for a time."

"Wow." She stared at him in the morning light filtering through the shutters over the table scattered with paper.

"You don't like the idea of me being a book-learner?"

"No, it's not that. It's just... where I come from you don't just change jobs. I left the country I grew up in to change my life. It was my one chance to change things. I guess I just believed that at some point – life would just resume in the same stuck way. Maybe I looked at it just as a better version of no-options. You came to Dellaweir to farm... to make a change. But it is like you believe you could go someplace else, do something different to make another change. I've never really thought like that."

"I like farming. I still want to do that. That's option one."

"Hmm, see – still an option.

Zach smiled as he stood and picked up his hat. It seemed like the first time he could remember that someone accused him of initiative without tardiness.

"Zach, do you know what I want? You said before I left, that I used to hum while I sew. I can do that anywhere. I just want to be home with you... that is *my* first option."

"Mine too." If this was what it was like to execute a chosen path, rather than passively submitting to a forced hand, then he liked the taste of it. Initiative didn't mean hasty though. And he went out to gather his horse.

22

Zach opened the door and ushered Tibby into Maurice Bailey's office. She sat in the waiting room and looked around. Zach had told her he had mended the table and the other projects on his list. When Bailey called them in, she stepped dubiously around piles of cluttered files, books, and loose notepaper on the floor. Tibby took a breath and focused hard on remaining calm. He peppered her with very frank questions, and she squirmed in the chair under his scrutiny of her disastrous sham marriage. Then they drafted a statement of her account, with a letter, filing for a Decree of Nullity with the Bishop. When the time came, they would go away to marry so that they didn't have to stand before Crowley to say their vows. They agreed a new routine would be forged into their week to work off Bailey's account as quickly as possible, including his fee for tutoring.

Before they left town, Zach took Tibby shopping for a new sewing kit and material. This time Tibby chose fabrics that were not just plain-weave to make up some dresses. They bought a bolt of calico or two as well. She had this attachment to the simple unbleached plain-weave now, and not just because it was serviceable. She had plans for a new dyed patchwork bedspread. Zach had chopped up the last throw and made it into a cover for Skitter's mat and a couple of horse-rugs. He couldn't bring himself to burn it along with the other stuff, but he wasn't going to sleep under it either. When the cart was loaded with supplies, they made their way back home. Tibby rocked in rhythm with the tread of the carthorse. It felt soothing, swaying her gently; the motion lulling away the pain and panic that had been her familiar companions. She leant her head on

Zach's shoulder and felt the secure reassurance of him being there beside her. This time, this time she was home.

"Don't suppose you would be up for a walk down to the lagoon in the morning?" asked Zach as he retired into his swag that night.

She raised her eyebrows and tried not to seem eager. "Oh, very well. I've heard it is the best chore in the day, and I am determined you will not have all the fun." It had been a long time since she had felt so light. Could something as frivolous and pleasurable as a swim not be considered a sin?

He sighed in relief and looked deeply into her eyes. "It is good to have you home Tibby. So good..."

In the morning he gently rocked her shoulder. "Good morning... time for the water cart."

She jolted awake and smashed him with the heel of her boot she dragged from under her blanket, catching the side of his face. "Keep away. I'm warning you!" she whispered hoarsely.

"Tibby! What?"

"Huh?"

"It's Zach. You clobbered me." He held his jaw as he turned away.

"Zach? Oh! My! Are... are you okay?"

"Wildcat," he muttered quietly, his eyes widening in a realisation. "I'm going out to hitch the cart." He walked out the door rubbing his chin.

She sat on the edge of the bed, massaging her temples in quick agitated strokes. She was confused; disorientated.

Zach stamped the dust off his boots and came inside. "Cart's hitched. Are you ready?"

"I... I didn't think since I... Zach I'm so sorry. I didn't mean too. I... well..."

He came over and held out his hand. "I'm guessing you didn't let him touch you without a fight. That didn't tickle."

She looked into his eyes. Why wouldn't he hold this against her too? Twice soiled. "I'm so sorry..."

"Come for a walk. You said you would come. Let's get some air."

She dutifully pulled on her boots. As she walked beside old Bob, the familiarity of his goaty smell; the puffs of dust that rose from the track as they walked; the trees and vegetation that was now sparse in the summer dry, all helped her to grasp that this was not a dream.

They stopped at the makeshift brick works in the clearing; crude pallets stacked up ready to take back to the house. There were rows and rows of the forms filled with drying slurry, and then lines of blocks hardening in the sun; standing like soldiers, ready to be deployed for service.

She stared. She hadn't wanted to believe his life had just gone on without her. Where did she fit now?

"Hey, I want to show you something..." He pulled her hand over to the stacked piles where one brick stood on top, like a sentry on lookout. He picked it up and handed it to her. Etched into the surface was a scroll emblazoned with a "Z & T" in the centre. "Bailey's got a book about architecture. The capstone is the block that holds the rest in place... mainly in arches. Or they insert a block near the foundation with an inscription that is a dedication of the whole structure. This is our brick, our capstone. This is what I came back to. You and me... holding it together. This idea helped me get through."

She held it in her hands and felt the weight of its meaning. "I had your promise. I held onto that like it would save my life. I guess that was my capstone."

"At the start... Tacko and Hilda... well I think they knew, that if they hadn't kept me drunk, I might have done someone harm."

She looked at him curiously. "You don't seem sorry for such a confession."

"I had to find a way to focus my rage. These bricks helped me do that." He searched her tired eyes and the dark circles that surrounded them, and yearning filled his chest that had ached for such a long time. He cleared his throat and tugged Bob's halter as they walked through the trees.

Tibby stopped dead and she stared at the lagoon. Zach had dug out loads of clay slurry, as he followed the receding water line towards the centre. The holey pits were giant boot-prints tracking a path through the jigsaw of a cracked claypan. Bob's wooden platform stood alone and bare on the edge of the dry basin. In the middle Zach had dug a well to access clean unground water, as the stock trampled the remaining water to a muddy slurry.

"Zach! What happened?"

"We haven't had rain. The locals reckon they've never seen this lagoon dry..." He shrugged. "Even in the massive 1864 drought it never went completely dry, so we've always assumed it was fed by a spring. The water from the well is still fresh... but the speed at which this has happened is a shock."

"It looks like a completely different place. Guess we won't be swimming anytime soon."

"The receding water meant I could make a lot of batches pretty quickly. But it dropped so fast. I don't understand..." He stared about him. He took Bob out onto the pan leading him around the dry mud pits, and filled the water cart from the well. It was a slow laborious job.

As he finished lunch that afternoon he looked over to Tibby. "Do you think you're up for another walk?" he asked her.

She pushed through her fatigue as they walked along the gravelly creek-bed. There were only a few areas where the creek stagnated in pools crusted with slime, but for large sections, where there had been permanent running water, now the surface was dry.

Cattle and wildlife left tracks as they made their way to those remaining puddles. Sections where moss and ferns had grown along the shady banks of the creek were now bare. Zach's brow furrowed. He monitored rainfall. This drought was extending past the other dry spells he had on record. That was true... but...

Abruptly he stopped, standing stock-still. A fence marked the boundary to Redwood Park. He could see piles of turned dirt and river stone that were used to stay posts. He stared at it for a while, and then abruptly turned to Tibby. "Stay here," he said as he climbed through the fence. Tibby sat down on the bank to rest and watched him disappeared around the tree-lined bend.

The warmth of the late afternoon lulled her senses. The birds were quiet for the most part, invisible amongst the trees, and occasionally they chirped a complaint. Suddenly she jolted awake. The sun was dipping low on the horizon and Zach was climbing back through the fence. A look of vile disgust burned in his eyes. She scrambled to her feet, and he grabbed her hand pulling her back down along the creek bed. His breath came in deep rasping gulps. Two more bends. Then he stopped; and kicked and flailed and cursed at the sky darkening in eventide. When they got back to the lagoon, he sat down on the landing, his face pale, his fists shaking, his eyes wild.

"Of all the evil, double-crossing, malicious, repulsive, pre-meditated schemes of treachery!" He put his head in his hands. "Unbelievable!"

His disgust shocked and confused her. She made herself sit down beside him, willing herself not to cry in shame. She would not turn away. Not now. Once their feet would have dangled just above the surface, creating circles in the water with their toes that would send ripples across to touch the other bank. Now they just hung listlessly in the air.

He swore again. "Bates has dammed the creek. A wall. The water's backed up. He's got a massive reservoir on his place. It's not just the drought at all."

"He's made a weir?" As horrible as it sounded, the relief of realising his anger was not against her felt like her own dam breaking. She calmed herself and focused. His breathing was rapid, his fists clenched, his lips pressed in an intense line. She had only seen Zach this fierce once before. Tibby blinked and shook her head. "How is this possible?"

"He's built it on his land. So, I guess he's entitled to do what he wants. It's quite a structure. It is..." He shook his head as if he really didn't believe what he had seen.

"But what about the other farms along the creek? Surely that's not right." She could feel his indignation in her throat. She found it hard to swallow.

"And yet he has." Zach felt his powerlessness acutely. There it was again. Someone with more brains, and more bread, and more brawn, just coming on in and taking whatever they wanted. Without water he had no farm. Without water, his years working here were worth nothing, or at least, barely a pittance. Without water, the herd he was building would suffer. Without water, it was all for naught.

He came in from his morning chores and sat sullenly at the table with his mug and breakfast. "Today is a Bailey day. I'll probably do more hours this week so I can clear off what's owed. Just as well, because I'm pretty sure I'll be not doing anything worthwhile here. I don't want you stay'n here alone, so bring your sewing... you can do it there."

Tibby sat and sewed, while Zack thumped around Bailey's office with brushes, rags, shellac, hammer, and nails. He finished a section of shelving and started sorting books according to Bailey's laboriously described cataloguing system. Tibby sat and stitched and tried to remind herself his anger was not against her. He clouted in another shelf, and Zach made a biting observation with every blow of the hammer. "For something... he's so damn... particular about... beats me... how... he... hasn't even... had... one book... on a damn shelf... this whole time! Strikes me... the floor... has done... well enough... up to... now!" Bailey disregarded his tantrums with ironic amusement and mildly asked for a certain text. When Zach couldn't lay his hands on it straight away, Bailey painstakingly went over the filing system again. Eventually Zach silenced him by finding him the book. That was his new reading assignment.

"I'm not sure I can keep going there," Zach said as they drove home that evening. To emphasise his disgust he added colourful, derogatory descriptors of Bailey's character, his family heritage, and his slovenly personal habits. "Said he wanted a clerk. Haven't even seen a ledger. If I'm going to be building and sorting things out, I got building and sortin' to be done at home. Haven't started your kitchen yet."

"Well, pay your bill and be done."

"Well, I'm working on it. That's what I'm doin'."

"Zach, you are not obliged to him, outside the services you hired him for."

"Huh. Except I don't reckon I'm getting what I paid for. Never laid eyes on the inside of any law-book."

"Well get it done and find someone else to do your book-learning with. Not sure you would find someone else with so many books though."

He grunted in disgust. "Not that he would know what books he has there at all."

"He knows. That book he asked for before we left: you couldn't find it, but he knew which volume he wanted."

"Tibby, are you saying I should stay on?"

"I'm not suggesting anything... except, you might be doing more for him, and more for yourself than you know."

"Humpf!"

So, over the next couple of weeks, the library was beaten into submission as more shelves were added, panels were painted with shellac stain, and sections were systematically filled. Tibby helped to sort the books according to Bailey's cataloguing system, making larger areas of the floor visible. Zach took notice of titles and authors, and became conversant with the collection, if for no other reason than the references Bailey asked for could be found with minimal pause, and minimal interaction. Even so there was always a pile of volumes left by Bailey beside his desk to be returned to the shelves every morning.

Zach poked his head into the office to sign out. He handed Bailey the sheet with the balance of hours from his account completed. Bailey shrugged and offered a sort of satisfied nod. "Well, it didn't take you long to regret domestic life. I'm a betting man and even I wouldn't have put a wager on that just yet. Do you still want to go through with it? Easy enough to withdraw."

"What do ya mean?"

"The annulment. You and her. Honeymooners are usually happier... for a little bit, anyways."

"Well, we ain't married. She's still married to someone else, so we don't get to do the honeymoon yet."

"Oh. Well, that explains a lot."

Tibby came and stood beside him in the doorway. "It explains what exactly?"

Bailey looked at them and shrugged. "Nothing. Nothing at all. Take the book and return it when you're done reading it."

Tibby swallowed and then blurted. "The neighbour stole our water. Is there nothing a law-abiding man can do to fix what is rightfully his?"

"Stole?"

"As red-handed as any coach heist," said Zach.

Bailey looked at him over the volume in his hand with raised brows, and by the time Zach had finished describing what he saw beyond his boundary fence, Bailey's eyes had closed to a narrow slit. Zach sighed. Of course, Bailey would be bored. But instead of retreating back into books, Maurice shrugged and asked Zach to retrieve a particular volume from the library. Zach shook his head in disgust. The man was as unfeeling as the stone-cold fish that were dying in his dried-up dam-pan. He impatiently got the book and slammed it on his desk and left.

"I like the man," said Tibby as they drove away.

"Well, I don't."

"He doesn't have airs. He has never pretended to be more than he is. He is a law-man who has issues with house-keeping and gambling. One he can't start; the other he can't stop. And yet he has always been respectful to us. He believed me. He didn't turn away when I told him what happened. That's one thing I know... lots of people turn away when you don't want to pretend."

He looked across at her. "You think I should keep going there."

"Why would you think that?"

"Because that's one of the biggest speeches I've ever heard you make."

She felt her neck flush with heat. "I don't see us as people who turn away, just because the man is not up for pretending either," she mumbled with downcast eyes.

He said nothing until they drove up beside the hut. "Thank you," he said sincerely as he secured the reigns.

"What for? I thought you were angry with me."

"Angry?"

"You haven't said anything for the whole trip home... so of course I thought you were upset."

"You are right: I am upset. But I'm upset about this Bates thing... not you. Tibby, not you. And yeah... not even Bailey." He reached over and placed his arm around her in an embrace, drawing her to him across the bench seat, like a magnet. "Tibby, you have more sense in your little finger, than most people have in their whole bodies."

This time her blush ran up into her cheeks. As clumsy as that compliment was, she felt valued, just for being herself... without pretending. With closed eyes she felt him near. He tilted her chin gently. Skitter came bounding out barking from under the verandah and she quickly turned away embarrassed and jumped down.

23.

When Zach opened the cover of the book Bailey had given him, he was a surprised to see that this time it was a law book. He resolutely ploughed through the strange syntax and complicated ideas. His purpose had not changed. He still needed to know the rules. The game was complex and persistent and exhausting. But none of that meant it was worth conceding. He was not one to yield. Not yet. Neither did he want to get side-lined because of ignorance or be disqualified from a technicality. He knew the maxim that ignorance was no defence in the law. He also knew ignorance was no servant. So, he pushed through and read on; a slow and laborious exercise. He spent a lot of time in the dictionary, which did not always help him understand the passages more clearly when definitions became a circular puzzle that coiled around in unsolvable loops. He would mutter away under the lamplight at night while Tibby continued sewing and she was comforted by his jolting monotone commentary of his reading which did not sound that different to the muffled dialogue he had with Skitter over the billy.

When he finished the book, they returned to Bailey. Zach looked around his office at the accumulated piles of references beside his desk. In the weeks they had been away things had deteriorated.

Bailey looked up with raised eyebrows as they walked in. "Haven't seen you for a while. Thought you were done, since your account's up to date," he said without ceremony.

"Brought back the book. Wondered if you might have another. I got a couple of hours should you need anything done."

"You read it?"

Zach shrugged. "Took a bit longer..."

Tibby stepped forward. "I want to do the chores while Zach does his books with you. That way we will be square, and he can cover more if he isn't scrubbing floors."

"It won't be enough."

Zach frowned. "She looks frail, but she works hard. You will get your pound of flesh."

Bailey looked her over, almost as if seeing her for the first time. "Okay then. Record what you do on this," and he handed her a sheet of paper. "Still, my fees will be more than that though.

"Why don't you just say outright if it you don't want to bother?" As far as value for effort goes, this was by far the dodgiest deal he'd ever come across.

Bailey raised his dark brows. "It's not the bother. This won't cover my professional fees that's all. I don't do discounts on them as a rule."

Zach glared. "You've just said we are squared away! It was agreed."

"To be sure. To be sure – the annulment is filed, and the tutoring agreement stands. But this other thing is going to be a fight."

"What other thing? What fight?"

"The fight of a law-abiding man doin' what he can... to fix what is rightfully his... when it's been stolen... red-handed..." He said it off-handed staring into the coffee cup in his hand as if he was not going to waste any opportunity to drink its contents, even when talking business. Then he raised his gaze and looked Zach in the eyes.

"Oh." The light behind Zach's stare changed from accusing to alert.

"There are regulations that protect landholders' access to natural water supplies."

"You think there is recourse about the water? But the dam is already built. On his land."

"But you are right. It is still your water, and just because it wasn't nailed down doesn't mean it wasn't stolen."

"You actually think we can fight Bates on this?"

"I think the fact that it is Bates gives the case a particular dimension that appeals to me. I believe we can put up a fight."

"You don't like him much." It was an observation.

"I got my reasons. He thinks he is above the law, and it would give me *great* pleasure to challenge that idea. But whether I like him or not is irrelevant."

"Okay then." Zach sat down opposite the desk. "Tell me where we start. I'll work at whatever you need to see this through."

Bailey nodded. He picked up a volume from the pile of paperwork in front of him. Zach recognised it as the book he had collected for him when he last left the office. "This book features one primary topic: Riparian Water Rights. This is where we start."

As he launched into talking through principles of English land titles and associated water rights, Tibby shrugged. "Well, I'll just get to work then." She collected the broom from the corner, dusted and

sorted books back onto the shelves. She lit the small pot-belly stove
and put on a fresh kettle of coffee. She opened the basket she brought
from home and set some pan scones on a tray with the coffee mugs
while they continued to talk through challenging the audacious and
criminal violations of neighbouring boundaries.

After morning tea, she washed up the tray and the other cups
and plates that had taken up residence on the sideboard. Then she set
to work to clean the street-front bay window and sills. Zach had not
touched the curtains, so she took them down to wash, and set to work
washing the dust off the glass panels inside and out. The glass shone
in the late morning sun.

When she picked up the curtains to take to the laundry, the
sun-faded fabric tore. They would never survive even a gentle wash.
She measured with a length of twine and arm's lengths what she
needed and went to Bailey to put forward her case for fresh material to
make new curtains. He held up his hand and Tibby swallowed.
Dismissed, she turned to go. But Bailey cleared his throat, continued
to make his point with Zach, with coffee mug in one hand, he and
reached into his drawer with the other and handed her a wad of notes
and a number of coins. "Use what you need," he said without
ceremony, and picked up the idea he was making with Zach with
barely a pause.

She walked out across the street, and down to the draper
shaking her head. The disregard Bailey had for money seemed
scandalous to her. He could have been handing her buttons. He had
no concern she could be uneconomical, or dishonest... and she wasn't

convinced he'd be too worried if she was either. She once had assumed the draper's supplies only consisted of calico and hessian, but after browsing for her dress fabric, she knew their range. Even if it was limited, she had in mind exactly what she wanted for the waiting area. She would get an extra length for cushion covers and a cloth runner for the low table.

She paid the amount and waited for the measured lengths to be wrapped in brown paper. The little bell tinkled when she opened the door, and abruptly she froze and quickly stepped back inside. Heather and Amelia were winding their way down the opposite side of the street in an imperial stroll. Heather nodded regally out from under the brim of her feathered hat that colour-matched her outfit perfectly. She sauntered along the street for maximum effect, condescendingly bestowing her presence with an outstretched hand, ignoring those who wore common attire.

It was about then that she saw Rupert Bates emerge from the bank in his brocade vest and well-cut jacket. Without pause he offered his arm to Heather who easily and comfortably took it with a gushing smile. Amelia faded into the background and Tibby watched the couple complete their walk with stately nods and royal smiles, as town's people bobbed and bowed in their wake.

Quickly Tibby gathered her parcel under her arm and dashed across the street and up the sidewalk to Maurice's little office. She rushed out the back and plunged into washing the un-shrunken fabric. Maurice lived above the office and his little detached bachelor laundry and bathroom block was rudimentary. He only had a temporary clothesline made of rope. As she rinsed out the soap, she shook her head in shock. She leaned over the concrete tub and felt her breath coming short rasping breaths. Heather and Mr Bates? Surely such an alliance could never be contested. Everything that Zach fought for would be ground down into chalky dust and tossed away on the wind. They shouldn't! They mustn't! They should go away! Go away!

"Tibby?" Zach touched her shoulder and she jolted, blinking hard in the bright light.

"What?"

"You were calling out. What's the matter? Did you see a snake?"

"I did? I did!" She shook her head, her eyes wide with fear. Should she tell him?

"Well, where'd it go?"

"Down the street." She stared at him fearfully. "Zach, I think Heather is betrothed to Bates."

"What?"

"I saw them... all cosy. I think they are a couple. We can't fight both of them!"

"My sister is hooking up with *him*?" She nodded with tears in her eyes. "Huh. Figured she'd give it a try. They deserve each other," he said. He looked at her pale face. "There was no snake hey?" She shook her head. He took a breath. "It changes nothing. We are still going to give it a shot. I'm not going to retreat just because they suppose we are from the same stock. They aren't family. There is no honour there."

"But Zach..."

"What?" His tone was short.

"You know what they are like. We could never win."

"Goliath thought he had that particular battle all sown up. He didn't count on the God behind the kid. We have that same God. I don't know how exactly, but intimidation is not to be borne. We are still going to fight."

24.

They walked back inside after Zach had strung up another clothesline so that the curtain fabric could be hung out to dry. They stopped silently in the back doorway as they noticed Maurice sitting behind his cluttered desk transfixed on something before him. They glanced around the doorjamb and saw Amelia staring around the office in amazement. "This place is so charming! Look at all these books. I've never seen so many books." She walked over to Maurice and gaped at him like some sort of holy man. "Do you read all these books?" she asked in whispered tones.

He nodded and eyed her blonde hair and soft figure. "Enchanting..." he said.

Her eyes widened. "You do enchantments? Are you some sort of wizard? I've heard of people like that... who live in libraries."

"I've just been put under a spell," he acknowledged readily without shame, his eyes not moving from her peach complexion.

"Oh! Is that bad?"

"No, not at all. I think *this* spell is the most powerful, intoxicating, healing potion I've ever partaken."

"Oh, excuse me, Sir, I did not use my manners. My name is Amelia. I saw Tibby come in here. I so wanted to say hello to her, because..." Her voice faded out in a tremor, and then she suddenly had an idea. "But perchance, I mean, if you are that sort of clever person perhaps you can help me."

The sun shone through a high window and spilt over her hair creating a golden aura around her. He swallowed and didn't think twice about misrepresenting his profession to involve spells and mystical remedies. He hustled around his desk and tipped off the files that sat on a chair sending them sprawling all over the floor. He offered her the chair quickly without taking his eyes from her face. "Please sit here and tell me all about it."

She blushed prettily; and then in hushed tones of distress told her tale. "Mrs Granger has organised me a husband. Mrs Granger said that she would find me a good type... like Zach. But I know that weren't... wasn't... meant to be. The one she picked instead is one of the stable hands. Well, a supervisor one... not just an ordinary hand. He's not a Breaker like Tibby's guy, and he looks nice enough, but the problem is... it's just that he ain't... he isn't... a good person neither. He sleeps with the kitchen staff and gets drunk when he's paid. He is just like Uncle Benny. He even sounds like Uncle Benny. I know I am supposed to do what Mrs Granger says, but he ain't... isn't... a good husband type. Aunt Agnes made me promised I'd do better than a Benny. But... he's just a Benny. And I don't know what to do. But then I heard the maids talking about how Tibby got away from her Benny type... and it made me think that maybe... maybe I don't have to do what Mrs Granger says neither, just because she says so. I ain't proud, not really, but I don't want a Benny." She looked up from twisting her gloves and tears glistened on her lashes.

"Marry me," said Bailey breathlessly.

"Why?" said Amelia quite bewildered.

"Because the best protection against an undesirable marriage is to be already married."

"Oh? That is so clever. I never thought of that."

"We don't have to delay. In fact, it would be expedient to act quickly in these situations... to avoid complications."

"Oh. Expeee...? Complications?" She seemed quite dazed. "But I don't know what type you are neither."

"I am your type, Amelia. Guaranteed."

She smiled and relaxed with a sigh, relieved that a great weight was lifted off her shoulders. "I would like to be married."

Zach stepped forward. "Hello, Amelia..."

"Zach? Oh!" Fear jumped into her eyes. She stood up quickly and stepped back. "I... I... saw Tibby... I just wanted..."

"It's okay," Zach said gently, soothing away her apprehension. "Tibby is here, and she would very much like to show you some fabric that she bought to make Maurice some curtains. It's out the back in the laundry... if you're interested?"

"Oh yes! That does sound interesting." She stopped and looked back at Bailey. "Maurice? Is that your name?" He nodded. "That is such a handsome name. Maurice..." She savoured the sound of it. He stared after her in a daze when Tibby quietly took Amelia by the arm and led her outside.

Zach turned on him. "Bailey! Are you insane? You can't marry her!"

"Pretty sure I can. She seemed agreeable to the idea."

"But she's..."

"She's a vision... that's what she is. And she thinks I'm clever."

"Amelia thinks rocks are clever. You're an attorney for crying out loud."

"I've got enough clever for both of us."

"You gamble. How are you going to support a family?"

"I'll reform. I am reforming... I already have! Done."

"This is a mess!"

"No, it's not. Look what you've done to this place. It looks great." He walked back and sat down behind his desk like a presiding judge in his courtroom. "Besides, she'll keep house. She said she isn't proud."

"I wasn't talking about your digs."

"I'm well aware I'm not the finest catch in the sea... but a stroke above Benny."

"Barely."

"Thanks for the vote." He paused, and then pulled from the drawer beside him a small square ring-box. "My heart was train-wrecked by an elegant, intellectual, well-to-do, ambitious woman. As far as smart goes, she was everything Amelia is not and that did not turn out well." He took his canister out of his pocket and took a light swig. "You've asked why I was so interested in your case. Well, the fact is she ditched me for Bates. She wanted the prestige of inheriting along with the son of the local baron. The mockery of it is that she died in childbirth after they moved out to Redwood Park. And he couldn't even give her and the baby a proper burial. She meant nothing to him." He took the ring out and held it up to the light. "I thought about hocking this dozens of times... but never could. Now it can be finally put on the hand of someone worthy of its price." He surveyed the ring in his hand and rubbed it on the corner of his shirt until it glinted.

"You are actually serious? You've barely met her! Think about this man!"

"Oh, I have. Would you want her to go through what Tibby did? That girl is an innocent. She deserves better than any Benny or Bates."

And that was the closing argument. Zach had to concede he had nothing to refute that.

25.

Tibby swept her duster over the desk again. Zach put the last of the files in the drawer and closed it firmly. Their unspoken commitment to the happy couple was that when they returned as Mr and Mrs Bailey, the restoration of order to the office would also be reflected in their living rooms upstairs. They did not want Amelia wading through piles of books and dirty socks to get inside their home. So, they budgeted the generous wad of notes Bailey had pressed into Zach's hand and swept and scoured and sorted and sponged and scrubbed and stacked and sewed solidly over the six weeks they were away to transform the Bailey hovel into a home. Tibby's sewing machine was constantly whirring. Curtains were hung in the upstairs bedroom and living room. A new throw was on the bed with matching pillow covers. Evidence of the bachelor was removed, flowers sat on the dresser, colourful cushions sat plump on the lounge. Zach installed a more permanent clothesline and scythed the pocket-sized back yard.

They made one final inspection before the newly-weds were expected home. As they gathered their things to make a quiet exit, they heard voices at the front door. A notice was posted on the window, announcing the unavailability of services for the duration of their extended leave. Just as they realised it was not frustrated clients, but the couple returning home from their wedding tour, the jangling keys were already turning in the lock. To avoid detection Zach quickly pulled Tibby into the kitchen alcove and squeezed in behind a hutch. It felt like she was playing hide-and-seek around the tenement houses of home. Tibby smothered a giggle, while Zach put his hand to his lips to encourage stealth.

Maurice surveyed the transformation; Amelia exclaimed her delight and ran upstairs with squeals of appreciation. Maurice stood at the door to his office and quietly mused, "You can come out now: the cats have been away, and the mice have been at play." When they didn't appear, Maurice chuckled good-naturedly. "The old tom and kitten were gorging on cream, sated with the adventure of married life so they are content and will not pounce." He cited all sorts of evidence that they were still in the building: boots by the back door; a dusting-cloth on the desk; a sweaty hat on the rack; a cup of warm tea on the sideboard. Sheepishly they emerged. They shook hands and their heads, astonished that the house wasn't the only transformation that was in evidence.

Amelia raced down the stairs and bowled Tibby over with a hug. "Tibby you are the best gem in the whole wide world! I hardly recognise this place. It will be so interesting to keep house. We have been away for ever-so long. You would never believe the interesting places we have been! We have stayed in the city and visited the country. We went to the mountains and to underground caves and the sea! Haven't I got the most wonderful husband in the entire world?" And she giggled and brushed his face with a kiss and flitted around the room amazed. After emerging from the cocoon of spinsterhood, no longer under Mrs Granger's guardianship, this was now her very own garden to tend. Maurice glowed and patted her indulgently. Happy couple indeed.

Heather stood in the doorway and stared at Amelia with loathing. Amelia trembled, unable to move under her scrutiny. Tears fell. Maurice came in the door with a file in his hand and quickly took in the scene before him. He threw the file on his desk and went to stand with his wife. "Amelia, why don't you go up to the bedroom hutch and sort my socks?" he said deliberately and quietly.

"Your socks?"

"Yes. I think they need... sorting."

"Oh..."

"Amelia, I'll call you if I need something."

"Okay."

She went away, climbing the stairs slowly. When she was out of sight Bailey turned to Heather with complete disinterest. He assessed the cut of her dress, the set of her lips, the frown on her forehead, the hiss in her voice.

She scowled with disgust. "Socks indeed! You are right enough to treat her like an imbecile. You have no idea what you have got yourself into."

Maurice said nothing, but the slightest rise of his brow launched her into another rant.

"She cannot be here because she is betrothed to another. She may have disappeared for weeks, and if that soils her reputation beyond repair and ruins her prospects, I will not be responsible. Foolish girl! Right now, she is still in my employ, and I will overlook the abandonment of her position if she comes back immediately."

"Generous. But I think she has resigned."

"That is not up to you, you arrogant little man! What right have you to make such assumptions?"

"I didn't assume. I asked her."

"You ignorant, horrid, disgusting little man! Do you think you know anything? Amelia has been with me for years! I plucked her from the most unsatisfactory circumstances and have groomed and moulded her. I know her like the back of my hand. I know what she needs!"

"Not too well it seems."

"Really! Amelia – get your things. We are leaving now!" When she didn't appear, she screeched louder. "Amelia!"

"I think you can go now and leave my wife alone," he said smoothly.

Heather choked. She stared at him in horror. "Did you say...? She cannot be married to you! I have already told you she is betrothed to another!"

"Look, I don't know what sort of scam you have got going: trading women with less consideration than you would a dog, but Amelia married me out of her own volition. She told me she had not made a commitment to anyone else, and she had serious doubts regarding your intended..."

"That is an outrageous lie! We had an agreement!"

"Well. Even if she had agreed, it is still her prerogative to change her mind. She is now under my household, and you are not to bother her again."

"You! You cannot do this! Amelia! Tell me that you did not do anything so foolish!" she said, livid with rage.

Maurice went to the door and opened it. Heather huffed and flounced her skirts outside onto the pavement. "You have not heard the last of this, you despicable filth!"

Maurice closed the door locked it and flipped over the Welcome sign. He climbed the stairs and found Amelia huddled next to the dresser, a box of socks in front of her, tears streaming down her face. "I'm sorry, I didn't sort the socks," she said trembling.

He gently pulled her to her feet and softly dried her eyes and soothed her brow, creased in frantic worry. "I don't care about the socks. Remember, we said that if I ask you to sort the socks, it is just a secret-code that you are to go and stay upstairs until I come and get you. You did everything perfectly. You are so brave not to listen to Mrs Granger make all those rude demands of you."

"She used such horrid words. She can be very mean sometimes."

"She might dress well with all her nice clothes, but underneath she is really just a Benny. A nasty bully."

"Oh... yes. I think you are right. I didn't realise. Aunt Aggie would have been very disappointed I picked up with a Benny... even if it was Mrs Granger." She sighed with the weight of her failure; fresh tears glistening on her lashes and cheeks.

"I think Aunt Aggie would be proud that when you found out... you got out."

"I did?"

"Yep... and you don't have to do anything she says... ever... if you don't want to."

"Oh Maurice... I think you are a very good husband type."

"And you, my beautiful Amelia... you are a very good wife."

She giggled and smiled through misty eyes, relief flooding her as he enveloped her in his arms.

Tibby put away the final pile of books on the low table now designated for return and went to check if anything else was required of her before she attended to some of her own errands before going home. Maurice stood up. "I do have something else I want you to do."

"Oh." said Tibby. Sometimes Bailey's list of chores was like a never-ending story.

"Actually, I want to propose something," he said. "An additional arrangement."

At that she raised her eyebrows. Zach looked up from the book he was reading and took off his eyeglasses. He said nothing.

"I would like to propose..." Maurice repeated and cleared his throat awkwardly. "... that to accumulate additional hours in paying the legal fees for which you have engaged my services, that you keep company with Amelia."

Tibby laughed. "You want to pay me to be your wife's friend? You don't have to do that!"

"She really is a nice person... and I would like to know she has some suitable genteel company."

"Oh. Well, I'm flattered that you think I qualify."

Amelia squealed from the staircase and came bowling over. "Oh goodie!" She laughed and wrapped her arms around Tibby's neck, "I knew you would say yes! Oh, this is so much fun! Thank you, Maurie. I knew you would convince her."

Bailey turned to Tibby with a plea in his eyes.

She smiled rather uncomfortably at Amelia's enthusiasm. "Sure... But just so I understand... if I keep company with Amelia after I do the cleaning, just like I have been already doing... that time will be taken off our bill at the same rate?"

He nodded and smiled indulgently on his wife.

Amelia jiggled excitedly. "Yes! And I get to choose. So, before this afternoon is completely gone, I want to go for a walk." Amelia picked up a paper bag, juggling her hat and parasol. Tibby shrugged and removed her hat from the hallstand. Amelia led the way out the door and turned at the street corner. "We are going down to the river," she said over her shoulder as she increased her step to a solid pace and Tibby had to skip a step or two to keep up. Abruptly Amelia sat down on a bench by the river and some ducks waddled over. She opened her bag and started throwing crusty dry bread at them with intense focus.

Tibby watched her for a time. "Amelia? What's going on?" Her frenetic duck-feeding didn't pause.

"I don't know what you mean. We are feeding the ducks."

"You are throwing bread at them like it is target practice."

"They all have to have a share. So, it is fair."

"I'm thinking this is not about the ducks. Did you and Maurice have a fight?"

That shocked her. "Fight? With Maurie? Oh no. Not at all. He is such a good husband."

"Doesn't mean you might not fight sometimes, or disagree..." That was a truth she understood now.

"Well of course not."

"Amelia? You do know that he wanted to pay me to keep you company? Isn't that kind of insulting?"

She turned and looked at her completely amazed. "Why? No silly! He knows I like you. It's his way of trying to help without seeming... you know, soft. This way we both get helped."

Tibby looked at her for a moment and marvelled at the possibility that Amelia might really be completely untainted, but not as oblivious to the realities of the world as she had supposed. She wondered why she had once been so jealous of Amelia and despised her simplicity. "So, everything is good with Maurice... and you're okay about me being asked to keep you company?"

"Of course! I like you, Tibby. You never pretend. Now we get to spend time together... and we can even help each other clean and keep house and it still counts. Mrs Granger used to pay me to keep her company, but I never thought that it was like a job. I really liked her. I thought she was smart and beautiful and important. But I never knew that... well, Maurie thinks she is a Benny. Am I really so stupid that I didn't notice what she was like? How could I not see that?"

"Oh Amelia. I like that about you: you always see the best in people. Heather has some good qualities... and you focused on those. That's a much nicer way of doing life than picking holes in everyone, thinking that they can't do anything right."

"Like Mrs Granger?"

Tibby nodded with a smile.

"Amelia, take command of yourself! Well don't just stand there, Tabitha – you are the help... so help! Zachary, you really are a naughty, thoughtless little boy," Amelia mimicked primly.

Tibby laughed outright. "See, you noticed exactly what she was like."

"I feel sad that she didn't really like me though. I thought she did."

"You could have been an angel from Heaven, and it wouldn't be enough for her to like. That is not because you are not likable... that is because she is not good at liking."

"Tibby? I was very upset about that morning tea. But I didn't know what to do."

Tibby's face clouded and felt panic knot in the pit of her stomach. "I know..."

"I am very sorry." Amelia's eyes misted with tears.

"I am too." She sat for a moment and realised she held no grudge against Amelia for her powerlessness in that moment. They were two women caught in a malicious trap. "Heather would not allow us to keep company even though we lived in the same house, but now we have found a friend in each other... and that is nice."

Abruptly Amelia stood up. She tipped the remaining crumbs on the ground and laughed as the ducks flapped and scrambled over them. "Well, you said you have some errands to do before you go home, so we can do those now."

"Oh, really, Amelia... you don't have to."

"But Maurice says I get to choose. I like being out. It is so much more interesting than sitting at home."

26.

It would have been the easiest thing to just to leave. There seemed no point working a farm that didn't have the water to support it. The price paid for Dellaweir was certainly beyond what it was now worth. Its value had seeped away as if trying to dam water in sand. Bates walked around town unashamed, arrogantly flaunting his brash disregard for conventions. Such rulings didn't apply to him. As time went on Zach had less and less hope that legal recourse would take effect, and he silently questioned whether continuing to work on their plans was worth it.

Zach sat on the verandah after returning from selling off most of his herd. He didn't want them losing more condition and market value. He had kept a few of his best breeders. The code of 'never-give-up' was unrelenting. Just plod on. Uncle Ced had taught him that every time they helped a cow to calve in the rain; or they fought to beat out bushfires; or rebuilt fence-lines washed out by floods. Every problem had a work-around, except drought. It was the deadliest of all. One could appeal to the grace of God against the dry, but it was a harder pill to swallow when it was not so much an act of God, but the brutal scheme of a well-to-do neighbour bragging about his invincibility.

The paddocks were turning from the colour of bleached calico to a dead sort of grey. It was a grim warning. Without the lagoon: no rain meant no water. It was living hand to mouth, and since Zach was in a habit of having some reserves in the pantry, this was hard to manage. Tibby came and sat beside him on the step.

"Do you reckon we should just go?" he said to her with a sigh.

"What do you mean?"

"Bailey has sent the letters; and he has submitted the application to the Lands Court, but I'm none too confident it will mean anything in a town that has been bought out by Bates."

"What happened to David?"

"David who?"

"David and Goliath. God fighting the battle. There were others in the Bible who did the same: fought against the odds... like Joshua and Caleb."

"Oh. Well, to be honest I don't think I've got any Joshua or Caleb or David left in me... I'm just one of the guys who felt like grasshoppers in the face of giants."

"But we talked about how those stories were not about how strong or even how powerless they felt. It was about how God could make up the gap if they let him. If we pull the pin, we lose all possibility of God intervening for us."

"Maybe. I really don't have the head for this particular giant."

"Zach, perhaps 'David and Goliath' is not the only way God fights our battles. I usually only think of the kid with a handful of rocks. But what if our battle will be won in a different way to a one-on-one stand-off with the villain? There are many other stories in the Bible of miraculous victories, with all sorts of interventions by God: flood, hail, marching bands, ambush strategies. Remember when we were reading in the Book of Kings about how the prophet Elisha saw the enormous Aramean army just abandon their post and they didn't have to fight at all. Wouldn't that be something? But regardless which way it comes, I will not give up praying for justice here."

"Justice is elusive. The court directive was clear enough, and Bailey's been patient explaining it, but it still is complicated."

"I'm wondering if you might not have the heart for it. Is it because Heather is part of this, that you don't want to stay in the fight?"

He looked at her quickly, but there was no bitter needling in her question. "Heather's actually a very good reason to keep going. She has a habit of working from the premise that right is only right if it benefits her. I reckon it would do her no harm to know that doing what is right is not always convenient."

"Well, I think you are right about one thing: her and Bates – they are well matched. She certainly did not waste time in solemnising that marriage."

"Quick marriages seem to be her speciality, outdone only by Bailey and Amelia."

He looked at her and gently frowned with a pensive smile. "You are the most provoking, annoying, sensible woman in the world. How could I be so lucky?"

"Zach, you know that I..."

He turned to her quickly and grabbed her hands. "Tibby will you be my wife?"

She grinned at him. "Wife? You were just accusing me of being annoying."

"I was hoping the timing would be better. I was holding out for some good news about our case. I saw Bailey today. He says it all just has to take its course. But I've been sitting here thinking that regardless of what happens here, I have one constant that I am confident of. That is you, Tibby. I didn't have an engagement ring when I asked before. Will you marry me?"

"Zach we can't spend money on a ring when you're selling your cattle. Shouldn't we be digging another well or something?"

"It isn't worth pot if you aren't mine."

"I am yours. You know that. But we can't do anything until the annulment comes through."

"Are you refusing me?" He pulled a little box from his pocket. "But..."

He knelt down on the step. "Tibby, I'm asking. Will you marry me? You have my heart. Will you wear my ring?" He opened the little box and presented a ring before her.

She shook her head in amazement. "Oh Zach... that looks really expensive. It is so pretty." She stared at it astonished. "This is for me?"

"Do you want it? Do you want me?"

"Of course!"

He slid it on her finger and smiled as he kissed her fingers. "I got you something else."

"You spent more?" She looked at him concerned. He handed her a small bound leather folder. She opened it up tentatively. Was he losing the plot? Had he really given up? "These are tickets... to the city," she said in a whisper.

"Well spotted."

"Zach, why? We can't give up and leave! You are not a city person."

"Don't want to live there. I just want you to come with me. On a holiday."

"A holiday? Have you completely have lost your mind? This is not a good time. I mean... things here are so unsettled."

"This is the best time in the world, because it is now. I don't want to put this off any longer."

"Zach what is going on? This is not like you. Shouldn't we save the money? Are you okay?"

He smiled. "I couldn't be better. This might explain..." He handed her another envelope. She opened it carefully and the paper trembled in her hand as she read the print. "Bailey gave me this today. It came through h. You are officially free. These tickets are so we can go away as we planned. It won't be a six-week tour like Bailey took, but we can get married. I don't care what else is going on. This is first."

She closed her eyes, her hand holding the envelope started shaking, and soon she was trembling all over. Tears fell blotting the envelope.

"Tibby... hush. I thought you would be pleased. You said yes... we said we would do this."

She shuddered in a sob and flung her arms around him. "Oh yes! I am pleased! We can finally be married." Even as she said it, she thought that was a stupid thing to say, because they were already together. Side by side. Grasshoppers against giants. After a while she pulled back and grinned through her tears. "This is a pretty short betrothal. These tickets are for Friday."

Zach handed over their bags to be stashed on the top of the stagecoach. He opened the door, and they stepped up into the carriage. There was only two other passengers and they settled into their seat. The driver flicked the reigns and called out to his horses as they flung their heads and moved forward. The coach lurched and groaned, creaking like an arthritic old man. Tibby looked out the dust hazed window and watched the town disappear. The rolling paddocks merged into miles and miles of untamed bushland. Scrubby trees overshadowed by mountains in the distance passed by and it felt like they were tracking through a wilderness to find home. They stopped at a nameless wayside stop and the horses were changed. Then they started again and somehow that felt safe, putting distance between those who were against them, and the hope that was awaiting them down the road. She reached out and held Zach's hand, and he almost didn't want to breathe from the leap he felt in his chest as he looked at her hand, wearing his ring, resting comfortably there almost without realising it. She was his.

They drove downtown and the driver called their stop. The harness jangled and creaked, and the horses lurched to a halt. They gathered their bags as they were thrown down. They hustled their way through the street, bumping busy commuters, noisy newspaper-boys and other hawkers trying to grab a stray penny from those milling around. They slowly made their way to the hotel overwhelmed by all the noise and energy.

Tibby stood in the foyer looking at the dark wood panelling and the grand motifs woven into the carpet. It felt like she had again stepped off boat into another realm, worlds away from reality. Funny how Dellaweir was now the only reality against which she measured all others. Zach paid the luggage-boy to carry their bags to the room while he spoke to the rather jaded clerk. Tibby followed the boy up the stairs. As he opened the door, she stood amazed by the soft furnishings, carpet on the floor and the grained wood-panelling all around the room. This time she was staying on the fancy side of the town bridge, not just delivering a parcel, and looking in from the outside. And then she noticed the bed.

Oh. One bed.

Then it hit her. If she could be married without that part... then this would be the most perfect thing. She went to the window and stared out across the rooftops of the town bustling below them. She felt afraid. Why should she feel frightened of the one person who loved, protected, and defended her? Zach came over and stood beside her and she felt herself jolt inside.

He didn't look at her. After a while he cleared his throat. "So now we are here. I have a plan... but I need your help."

Tibby smiled. "Let me guess, you have a lady visitor coming and you would like help setting up the hotel room."

"Sort of... except – I have a wife coming. And I really do need help..."

She relaxed. "Your wife sounds like trouble."

He looked at her and smiled. "So much trouble. I love her very much and I'm terrified I'm going to mess this up."

"How could you possibly mess this up?" Did he see her fear?

"We go to the church on Monday. But that is only one part of being married."

"Oh." She felt her throat constrict.

He watched the shadows cloud her eyes. Yes. He had been right about this. "Hmm. Terrifying. I need help in creating the biggest distractions possible," he said lightly. "So..." he pulled out a bunch of flyers. "I wondered which of these would be most distracting for the lady concerned?"

"Distracting?"

"Here is a boat ride around the harbour; or we could have a picnic at this 'pleasure garden'. They have some rather strange and exotic animals there, like an elephant and a Bengal tiger. I've never seen those... thought that might be distracting." He laid out cards depicting the beach, museums, and art-galleries. "All for our distracting pleasure."

Tibby sat down. This was for her to choose? "Well. I think the picnic with the tiger is a definite. And I would like to go to the beach. My cousin spoke of a holiday at the sea-side once and I've always wondered what that would be like."

"Wonder if it is as they say... that floating is easier in saltwater?"

"Oh, I wasn't thinking of swimming."

"I was. That's the best part."

They ate dinner from newsprint staring at the waves washing along the beach. It was a dream of a day, dazzling her breath away. She was completely fascinated by the tiger, terrified by the elephant ride, and dazzled by the fan-tail of the peacocks strutting around the pleasure garden. As they walked back to the hotel, under the flickering streetlights of town, they laughed about the antics of the monkeys. All too cute. And very distracting. Zach opened the door to their room and the laughter died on Tibby's lips as she looked at their room. It had been so distracted she'd forgotten the dilemma of only one bed.

Zach said nothing but went to the cupboard and pulled out a blanket. "Another night in a swag for me," he said casually. "Thank you for a very entertaining afternoon. While you sleep on the comfort of your mattress you can be planning your preferred distractions tomorrow. Good night, Tibby." He rolled onto the lounge and pulled up the blanket.

27.

Tibby eventually dozed off to the street sounds below them. Noisy revellers from the pub sang bawdy ditties and occasionally she heard something smash in the streets accompanied by yelling and swearing and a dog or two barking. When she woke, Zach was dressed in his suit, sitting at the table reading the newspaper with his eyeglasses on. The table was set with breakfast and a cup of coffee. He smiled as her eyes took in everything around her.

"Good morning. Did you dream of your preferred distractions for today?"

"Oh." She rubbed her eyes and self-consciously reached for her shawl.

He stood to his feet. "I'm going out so you can have breakfast and get ready. Will be back in half an hour... so think about your plan for today."

He took longer, and when he came in, she was staring out the window at the bustling street traffic below. "So, Miss Flanders, what is your distracting pleasure this morning?"

"I'm really not that good a choosing such things." After such a perfect day, would another be totally disappointing? She almost didn't want to tempt fate.

"Huh. I thought yesterday had extraordinary examples of distraction. Monkey tricks and peacock tails."

"Okay. Well. I would like to try an iced drink from the vendor by the beach we saw yesterday..." All of this felt so fraudulently extravagant. She picked up a flyer of a natural historical museum and the art gallery. "Perhaps see some of these galleries. I saw a painting once in the house of a lady who ordered some drapes, and I wondered what it would be like to step inside the picture. There were some sheep in the greenest field. It was so different to what I have ever seen, and for the longest time I imagined running on that green grass. I wonder what other places might be in such paintings..."

Zach smiled. "Who would have thought my practical Tibby had such a whimsical side?"

"Oh. Well. You pick something else then. I told you I was not good at this."

"Why pick something else? Whimsical sounds like a perfect distraction. I'll need help with the imaginative part, that's all. That is why I asked you along... consulting in all things domestic." He picked up his hat. "Today we have a gallery to visit, and iced treats to try."

They stepped inside the hall holding their tickets a little awkwardly. A gaggle of ladies were standing with their parasols and fans waving in the heat. They looked the couple over, and noted their plain attire, and stretched their long necks in disapproval. Zach just nodded and walked past tipping his hat, "Good morning to you, Ladies," he said without turning.

"Do you think we should go?" whispered Tibby.

"But how will you see your whimsical paintings if we leave?" he whispered back with a level of mischief as he took his hat from his head. "We can pretend they are a portrait of another world where we may never want to live, but today we have paid so we can stare while we visit."

Tibby giggled. "Zachary... in this one moment I might agree with your sister. You are being naughty."

They wandered around, amazed at the skill that created another world in each frame. They stood in front of a painting of a cow with large brown eyes standing in mud and straw by a barn. They considered what it would be like to be the maid in the cap who was responsible for milking her: was she a good-tempered cow or a temperamental milker? They noticed the trees and the clouds and speculated whether the season was hot or cold.

They spent time at another painting of a cluster of fine ladies and genteel men dressed like dandies flirting around a fountain. Tibby thought of another fine parlour on the other side of the world. "These dresses are made of silk. You can tell by the way the light shimmers on the folds. So pretty. Feels so fine."

Zach tilted his head. "I think this bloke is a sap. Look at the way he curls his hair and is falling over himself to be noticed. He's bored. A solid days' work would do him good."

"The lady's hands are so white. She hasn't done an unpleasant task in her life. Her problems consist of tuning her lute or choosing her embroidery thread colours."

"There are so many flowers in this painting. They are growing out of the pavement and water fountains."

"Perhaps the artist thinks being in love is like that and wants their life to always be spring, full of beautiful things, music, sweet smelling flowers, singing birds."

Zach laughed. "But all together it's so insipid. No substance... no strength. One hot day and the whole thing wilts and shrivels. I prefer a love that's tough. Like my Tibby."

Tibby blushed, turning away quickly, she pointed to another painting. "Look, this could be our lagoon. Zach, this could be you standing in that little boat... me on the platform."

His face went still as he looked at the man standing in his vest and britches, sleeves rolled up, gazing at his maiden. "Did I look like that on our water barrel runs?"

Tibby blushed again and giggled at little. "Oh no. You were never so well dressed."

Zach looked at her curiously, her blush intensified, creating hope in him. He bowed gallantly. "Me-Lady, would you like to come now and search out iced-wonders?" And without waiting for a reply guided her towards the exit. Instead of wandering through the bush to the lagoon searching out curiosities in the light of dawn, the streets became their landscape. They pointed to the pigeons perched on rooftops like kings; the texture of imposing sandstone façades; the light glinting off windows; cut down barrels used as planters for a stray flower and an abundance of weeds; and the grubby faces of children playing in the allies behind the public houses.

As they came to the beach, the vendor's cart was not on the corner where it had been yesterday. Tibby sighed. "Oh. No matter. It was a silly fancy after all."

"Silly is the point of distractions. Well, now we have a mission to find a suitable alternative." And he followed the sandy walkway back to the street. They wandered around, taking in various sights until Zach, with a determined step, steered Tibby's arm towards a café. He seated her inside, Tibby's eyes widened. Zach flicked his serviette comfortably onto his knee.

"How can you be easy in this place? It is so fancy," she whispered.

"Fancy enough to be a distraction?"

"Oh, I'm thinking so. I can hardly breathe..."

"You forget that I spent every Christmas of my life in the company of Aunt Peony who was a stickler for fancy rules. Apparently, all that seasonal anguish had its uses. A place like this is not my preference – a stump and a fire does me, but I can hold my own if I need to." He cleared his throat and put on his eyeglasses to read the menu board and winked. "What interests me are the drinks and deserts. They have ice." And he ordered iced cream in a cup. Tibby tasted it with wonder. Together they sipped an ice-cold drink through a straw; and finished off with chocolate fudge. She had never tasted such wonderful treats.

As they stepped outside in the afternoon glare, they stopped on a corner where a busker was playing a tuba spewing fire from its bell, in time with his rhythm box that he kept beat with a pedal. Zach dropped a coin into his hat.

Tibby felt like every one of her senses had been indulged. She wondered how she could capture those ideas into a quilt, pieced together like a story-board. On the way back to the hotel Zach asked her to choose which had been her most memorable distraction. She refused to demean the others by selecting just one.

At the foyer, Zach collected a large box and carried it up the stairs. He handed it to Tibby as she sat on the chair. "This is for you. Another distraction."

She opened the lid and there was a very simple white dress that fell in soft folds to the floor, as she held it against her figure. "Oh Zack! It's beautiful."

"I'm sorry you didn't have time to make your own wedding dress. That would probably been much more to your liking. But I wanted you to have something nice to wear to the Church. And then if you like, you can dye it to wear again later."

28

Tibby knocked on Ol' Hilda's hut door. Tacko was sitting at the table with a mug in his hand in that half-dozing inertia that comes after a full day's work. Hilda looked up from her mending in the lamplight. "What are you doing here, Girl, in the middle of the night. Where's Zack?"

"At home. We are married now."

"Heard that." Ol' Hilda looked at her and put down her mending. "Tacko, them horses are stirring, restless like... you'd better go and check on them," she said without turning her head.

He looked up from his mug to object, and then scrapped back his chair and silently grabbed his hat from the stand. He never went outside without it, noon or midnight.

Hilda indicated a chair and poured a drink from the kettle. It was past tepid, but it was the gesture that was needed. Tibby took it wordlessly. Hilda sat and said nothing.

Eventually Tibby put down the cup. "He loves me. I know that. But I can't."

With the instincts of a woman, there was no need to clarify exactly what she couldn't do. "Can't? Or won't?"

"I don't know!"

"Seems to me that you do."

"I want to be his wife... but just not that. Perhaps I don't love him after all."

Hilda shrugged. Not scandalized. Her indifference to the topic made it seem less shocking... more regular, routine. "Comes with the territory. Have you at all? Ever?"

"With Zach?" Tibby shook her head. "No... that time you came to tend me... that was not Zach." She shuddered and went pale. "It happened on the way here... I tried to run... but he knocked me down. I don't remember much... except the pain."

"So, you reckon it is always like that? It ain't you know."

"After the wedding vows, I asked to come straight home. We have slept in the bed... but not... anything else."

"He didn't make you?"

"Zach? No, of course not. He would never."

"Then Girl you need to make that move. You ain't married until you do it. That paper means squat. You need to consummate this marriage."

"Huh. You said you had no head for legal stuff."

"I also told that maniac you were plum-crazy. What I do know is that I have never seen someone so determined to get back to a man. Girl, love's not the issue. You just have to do the next thing. Hard as it is."

"But I don't want to lie. I know what it means to him, but I can't pretend I'm okay with it."

"Then why are you here?"

"I thought maybe you had a potion or something... that would change the way I feel."

"Wouldn't that be something?" She left that idea hanging.

"You do then? I will pay you."

"Look, Girl. You are tough. You don't need no remedy. You just need to do it. They told me when I got married that it was a woman's duty to get through it. My first husband was nasty and rotten to the core. Getting through was all you could do. It was never that way with Tacko. He's not a mean sort."

"I don't know how to... you know... get through it."

She paused. "Ever been a time when you were not thinking so reserved with him?"

Tibby blushed. Bare chested.

"See. Now that is what I'm talking about." She stood to her feet. "You do this or all that play-acting you did in that hut over there will be for naught."

Tacko came back with his horse and on Hilda's instruction he rode her back to Dellaweir. When they rode up, Zach was sitting on the verandah, staring at the stars with an unreadable look in his eyes. Tibby jumped down and went around the back without saying anything. Tacko dismounted slowly. Zach swallowed and there was a catch in his voice. "I thought she'd done a runner."

"She ain't never had a mother type to talk to. She needed an Ol' Hilda moment; that's all."

"I didn't expect it to be like this. We've been home for weeks."

"Bought a filly once... for a song. Good bones but beat up terrible bad. Some stable hand just figured he would bash her into line. They broke her... but not for the saddle. In the end they couldn't do anything with her. Took a while, but she came good... but always was a bit skittish like." He paused. "Don't you give up now. Ya done all the hard work."

When Zach came inside Tibby was in her nightdress sitting at the table. He looked at her and swallowed as she stood up tentatively.

"I wondered if you would sleep on the swag tonight. Like you used to. I'll take the bunk." Her bunk was made up and the spread folded back.

"Tibby? Should we be going backwards? This is not the way it is supposed to be."

"I know. I just..." She didn't know how much she could say.

"But Tibby..." The frustration in him was ploughing through work with a remarkable level of methodical efficiency. The kitchen pavers were all laid; the brickwork around the hearth was finished; the uprights in place; the stones sorted for placing. It was a speed record that Zach's history had little to compare with. It was not the honeymoon he had been hoping for though.

"Please..." She looked away.

He shrugged resigned. It felt like he was being strangled from the inside. He grabbed the blanket and pillow off the main bed and threw them on the floor. He had convinced himself that he had done his time; that all the rough, hard, lonely nights he had to endure were over. So, what was another night? Or was it to be a lifetime of roughing it, alone on the floor? He didn't take off his shirt, but just pulled up the cover and tossed uncomfortably.

Her heart sank and she rolled over on her bunk and tried to think what else to do. This was her plan, but now he was just irritated with her. She rolled over again and looked at him in the moon lit shadows. He was staring at the rafters, the rug twisted awkwardly. He wished for the amnesia of sleep. His muscles were tired from work, but sleep eluded him. Finally, he got up and had a drink. Before he went to lie down again, he sighed, took off his shirt and tossed it on the chair. He straightened the swag to make it more comfortable and laid down again. He lay there looking at the ceiling. Wakeful.

Even when he eventually closed his eyes, she could tell he was not asleep. Did he know she was not asleep either? She looked at him lying there on his swag. The man leaning over his books adjusting his eyeglasses was unfamiliar. The man in the fancy café, flicking his serviette onto his lap, was a stranger to her. The man lying still in the elegant hotel bed beside her was weird. But this... this was her Zach. There was a time when she had not been thinking reserved thoughts about *him*. The simplicity of roughing it was effortless for him. This was the man she fell in love with: the man in her dream who gently kissed her forehead; the man who hewed timber with an adze and built simple furniture; the man who taught her to float in the billabong; the man who protectively knocked teeth out for her.

In the silver shadows of the moonlight, she got up and lifted his cover and lay down beside him. She put her head on his bare chest and listened to his heartbeat. He lay still for a moment, scarcely able to breathe as he felt her close. And when he gently tilted her face towards his, their kiss was not awkward. Husband and wife.

29.

Tibby stood in the doorway and watched Zach at his books. She rubbed her abdomen, large with their baby and she wondered what sort of world they were bringing their child to. Justice had evaded them. Although the Lands Court ruled in their favour, there seemed to be no recourse to enforce the edict of a legal tiger that sounded fierce and yet had only paper teeth and no bite.

Heather finally ruled supreme at Redwood Park. She had effectively evicted Mrs Novak in a domestic political manoeuvre that raised many a brow and established her reign. And then another brow-raising moment came. They had a visit from Tacko and Hilda.

They sat in their new kitchen area looking over the bank of trees at the back while Tibby served tea and damper. Eventually Hilda pursed her lips in a definite line. She turned and spoke to Zach. "So, what's ya gonna do when the gurung comes?"

Tibby sat down in her chair, fatigue seeping out through her eyelids. "I can take care of our baby," she said defensively.

Zach would hear Hilda out. "We are prepared to look after our own. I reckon you know that, so what are you getting at?"

Hilda kept her gaze firmly on Zack. "You got a girl who looks like a puff of wind would blow her over; with that and a farm, ya gonna need help."

Zach sort of snorted. Not disrespectfully. "We'll manage. Have to. Labouring these days comes at a premium. Half the district's cleared off to the goldfields. Even Bates is struggling to keep his blokes." He glanced over to Tacko. "Thought you might give it a shot. Got to be better than where you are."

He chuckled. "I got problems but gambling with a gold-pan ain't one of them. But then again; what Hilda's proposing is gamble enough."

Zach chuckled. "Proposing? I thought you were just reminding us life is hard. We're familiar with hard."

Hilda put down her mug. "We done our time at Redwood. Bates bonded Tacko to pay his passage to get him here. That's done now. We want to work with you; help with the gurung when he comes."

"Here?" Zach blinked. That was direct. He looked at Tibby. "Perhaps, if I had more stock, I probably could've put on an extra hand... but I just don't have the water to support that many head of cattle now. I haven't got the work."

Tacko just looked into his mug. "You got the work. Just mightn't have the pay."

"One and the same. If you're working for me, I gotta pay you."

"Getting out from Bates is a start I'm willing to take as payment." Tacko looked at him straight. "We want to put together our own place. You portion us off a plot... hut, rations... cow, chooks... that kind of thing. We work for the cost of it all."

"How much of a 'plot' do you want?" When he answered Zack looked over at Tibby, "What do you reckon?"

"Well, I don't know. It's your farm."

"Actually, since we're married, it's our place. I need your opinion."

"Well, I don't have one," and she quickly got up and filled the kettle with water. When she sat down, she swallowed hard, picked up her needle and went back to stitching a wrap for the baby.

"Hmm." Zach turned back to Tacko and Hilda. "I'm inclined. I'll give it some thought and sort through the numbers. When I've got it worked out, we can get together and you can see if you're still keen on the idea."

As they watched them leave, Tibby stood on the verandah. "Bailey's rubbing off on you. Once you would not have worried too much about the details and just done it," she observed.

He shrugged. "Maybe. Tibby, this affects you: our baby, our family. I need to know what you think."

"How can I have an opinion on something I don't understand. It's not that I don't want to. I just think it is unfair to ask... especially in front of people."

"I never intended to embarrass you."

"Well, if it was the type of fabric in making Hilda a dress, I'd have opinions a plenty... but this stuff? Zach, this is your domain. I just can't make it up. I know you won't do anything to jeopardise our family."

"I've always gone solo. You changed that, but I'm not sure we have space for others here as well. But Ol' Hilda makes a valid point – we need help."

"Well... I think these are good people who would stick by their word. They'd never be disloyal. That is worth more than anything."

"That's an opinion I respect."

They talked about options to section off a parcel for Tacko and Hilda. Zach would not compromise on the basic aspects of privacy and space. A block that ran back towards the creek seemed like a doable option. The well in the drying lagoon bed would have to supply both households. Zach ran over the deed and details with Maurice and filed the appropriate documents with the Lands Office. They signed the documents sealed with a mug full of Hilda's precious homebrew.

The idea of having regular man-hours at their disposal suddenly opened up a whole lot of possibilities. They started an extension for the baby's room, and a larger self-sustaining vegetable garden. Tacko and Hilda lived in a small makeshift donga, and when they started pegging out their hut, Hilda stood presiding over their site like the matriarch of a great kingdom. Tibby went and gave her a hug. "We are neighbours now."

Tibby sat nursing the baby. Since Millie Francis made her harrowing entry into the Logan household they had settled into a simple routine. Ol' Hilda had delivered the baby, and now Tibby was regaining her strength and her determination. Zach read to them in the evenings, and regardless of his work routines, he hovered protectively over his little family with pride. He came in for lunch and smiled as Millie's rosebud lips puckered in a cupid's bow dozing off in Tibby's arms.

There was a knock at the door. Zach answered it and stood in the doorway silently. After a short pause he said icily, "You are not welcome here."

"Oh, Zachary. I am family. I have come to make amends and repair some bridges."

"Blowing up bridges with gelignite is more your style. What do you want?"

"Why do you always assume I want something? Can't I...?"

"Because you always do. So, tell me what your agenda is, Heather... or leave. It is simple enough." He made no move to invite her inside.

"Very well." Heather craned her neck to peek inside. "My niece?"

Zach moved across to block her. "Heather... I'm warning you."

"Well, alright then. Everybody has gone. The discovery of that new gold strike is close enough to tempt the staidest of hands. There is no one left. Ran like rats abandoning a ship. Even Rupert got gold-dust in his ambitious beady little eyes. Can you believe he's joined The Rush? He is delusional. He says this is the answer to his debts. He seems to think that nuggets are lying around just for the picking." She wrung her hands in disgust. "He expected me to go with him! Living like vermin in whatever hovel they can slap together! It makes your grotty little humpy look like a castle."

"Ahh," said Zach without emotion.

"What do you mean 'ahh'? Have you no sympathy for the outrageous plight I find myself in?"

"No not really. It has a fine sense of justice in a way. Good day Heather."

He went to close the door, but she barred it with her boot. "Wait. I want to propose something."

"I have no interest in your proposals, Heather. They generally do not work out well."

"But not this time. I'm leaving. Redwood Park is a ghost town. I can't stay. I won't. I deserve better..." She paused and tried to reword it, so it didn't sound like this was just about her. "Rupert could be lying in a ditch somewhere. I would have no idea whether he is dead or not."

"Tragic. It has nothing to do with me."

Heather quickly pushed the door back again. "So, I am going. And... it is incumbent of me to do what I can to ensure the resources at Redwood are managed... appropriately... indefinitely." She raised her eyebrows and nodded.

"Heather, would you drag me into your small-minded nasty little plot for revenge against your husband for leaving?"

"Why not? Like you said: justice. I've been doing some digging around myself. The place is not freehold. You take over the Redwood lease. Of course, there would be remuneration for personal items... equipment... enough for my personal maintenance back in civilisation. Let's face it: things have not gone well for you since the weir was installed. This would give you access to permanent water in a drought. This is an opportunity to live in a place more in keeping with a Logan. Have your daughter grow up with dignity."

"Millie will be fine growing up here. We are not sub-leasing to Bates. And we are not moving to Redwood Park."

"Why ever not? The house is fair..."

"No sub-lease. We are not moving."

"Well, you don't have to move there... take over the lease, in full. No sub-let. It is long-term... at minimal rates." In a hurry she volunteered her intention to seem reasonable. "You could get that weaselly little lawyer friend of yours to oversee the transfer... write up the contract."

"You don't have authorisation to make such an offer. You are just a wife."

"I know people who can rubber-stamp it. Things are more liberal now that anyone and everyone are migrating to the fields. Besides, a forsaken wife... destitute... living like a widow, looking after our derelict property falling into disrepair... pressed upon me in cruel and undeserved circumstances... There is justification there. And, you are family." She pushed a leather document pouch into his hand. "Some papers... so you can see for yourself that what I offer is legitimate."

"I'll get Bailey to look at it on the condition that the dam comes down. The Court ruling is to be complied with."

"Well of course... that would be legally responsible."

"And yet responsibility – legal or moral, was never on the agenda before."

"Zachary – there are some matters in which a wife cannot meddle, as you so rightly observed. But an abandoned wife... a widow in all practicality... well, necessity allows a little more say."

"Heather. My gut is telling me your schemes are trouble." He sighed. "I'll talk to Bailey like I said. If for no other reason than to get our water back."

"Well Lady Luck has had her say. Just don't be tardy. I am leaving at the end of the next week." And she twirled and left, walking down the track in the dust.

Zach watched her pass the treeline at the creek-bed with her parasol swaying in the breeze and disappear out of sight. She really must be all alone if she had to walk over here. He thought about hitching the cart to drive her home... and then shrugged and walked back inside.

Maurice went over Heather's proposal and drafted up a series of documents. Zach took him out to Redwood Park to investigate it further. While they were gone, Amelia visited with Tibby, doting on little Millie with gentle affection, clucking like a chook over a clutch of chicks. "Tibby... do you think that I could ever have a baby of my own?"

"Of course. Why would you doubt such a thing?"

"Well... it's just... I know we don't need much... and if it was a girl, perhaps we could manage in that little place... but a boy? Where would he run, or ride, or do boy things? It seems such a very small house for a family." Living above the library and office was kind of cosy as a couple but the idea of a baby, or a toddler, or a growing child... just didn't seem to fit.

"Would you like to have a baby?"

"Oh yes, of course. It would be so much fun. I would call a boy Hamilton Maurice Bailey junior. That sounds so very important. He would be so clever like his father. A girl... well, I couldn't decide but Maurie thought that Eloise Amelia would be as pretty as a picture. Having a girl would be so interesting."

Tibby looked at her and raised her brows, and then glanced at her figure. "Amelia... are you... well... are you already in the family-way?"

"Well... I could not be sure... but the womanly... you know... they have stopped. But I know that I am not because I feel perfectly fine... and I haven't got any sickness. Aunt Aggie was always pregnant... and she would be so very sick. And you were so unwell to start with... but I am not at all, and I was hoping that I did feel terrible... because then I would be completely sure... but without the sickness... it can't be that. Can it?"

"Not everyone feels sick," said Tibby with envious acknowledgement.

"Really? I didn't know that. Could it be... you know... that I am?"

"Perhaps. How long since your last flow?"

"Oh grief. I do not know... but it has been forever. Well, a while anyway. At least since little Millie was born. Maybe earlier."

"Millie is four months old. Have you felt the quickening... when the baby moves?"

Amelia stared at her amazed. "It moves? Early on? Aunt Aggie let me feel little Horace just before he was born. I used to call him Horrible Horace because he was so much trouble for Aunt Aggie. I thought him moving like that was just him causing his mother problems, being like his father."

"It starts like little flutters. Later, Millie used to do somersaults, I am sure."

"Oh..." Amelia quickly sat down as something was dawning on her. "Oh... I thought I was nervous sick about how a baby could grow up in a library. Maybe it is not butterflies, or worry... but... oh! This doesn't mean the baby's a Benny does it?"

"Does Millie look like a Benny?"

"Oh no... she is an angel."

Amelia thought despairingly of the little loft that was their bedroom and living quarters. "Do you think Maurie will think I am being needy if I tell him it is not really a family house?"

Tibby thought that when it came to Amelia, she could ask Bailey for a castle with a moat, and he would deem it especially reasonable. "I think he would be reassured that you are a caring mother."

"But Tibby, I have so much. How can I ask for more?"

"Explain what concerns you. Maurice is an intelligent, considerate man. I'm sure he would want to help if you just let him know."

"Oh, you are right. He is a very clever, thoughtful person. I am a terrible wife to doubt him."

"Or perhaps you are just getting used to what it is like to talk about these problems together."

It was about then, that the door opened, and Zach and Maurice walked in with Tacko and Hilda. They all settled in for a cuppa with sober looks and a wad of papers. Tibby took it all in. She didn't want Heather interfering in their life again. The fear of that thought was suffocating her. She hurried away to change Millie's nappy. Hilda got up and went after her.

Amelia poured some tea, but she didn't leave as she normally did when the men were trowelling through their books and documents. She cleared her throat and looked wistfully after Tibby and Hilda, hoping very much that they would not be long.

"Amelia? Are you okay?" Maurice asked.

"Oh yes, I believe so. I have been visiting with little Millie all day and she is such an angel and so very smart. She can hold things in her chubby little fingers. I thought she was even going to roll over!"

Zach thought this time Amelia astutely assessed the situation. He also believed his daughter was very clever.

Maurice tilted his head and looked at her. "You look worried my dear. What is causing that frown on your pretty little forehead?"

"Oh Maurie, I have been thinking about what it would be like to be our own little family. I know a baby like Millie does not do much, but what would happen when they grow and want to run around? It is so cramped in our little place; how could children to do normal growing things? And they would be getting into all your important books. And Tibby said that it would be good to talk with you about it because you are clever and have such good ideas.”

Maurice smiled at his wife. And then glanced meaningfully towards Zach. “See? My wife appreciates my capabilities... and you would also do well to learn not to doubt me.”

Zach went to respond... but silently took a drink, with a nod instead.

Maurice pulled Amelia into his lap and she giggled as he soothed her brow. “Amelia dear. You make a very important point. That is a work office... and although a loft makes a great little honeymoon nest... you are right: it is not a family home. I think a larger house would be much more fitting for my beautiful wife and our family.”

She giggled again. “Oh Maurie. You are so kind not to get impatient with me. Although I do love our little love-nest.” She caressed his face as if nothing was beyond his capability and she fully believed he could conjure up a house with a flick of his very clever quill. She whispered, disclosing her very shameful secret. “I was very frightened to tell you. I do not want to seem ungrateful because you are a very good husband to me. But Mrs Granger... I mean Mrs Bates; she said I am very needy sometimes... and it is not like I mean to... I just...”

“Amelia my dear... you are not needy... you are adorable. And I think you will make a wonderful mother.”

“Oh!” she squealed delightedly. “I am so glad you think so, because Tibby thinks I might be in the family-way already and I am so frightened to get excited in case it isn’t yet!”

And Maurice landed on his feet and spun her around with great enthusiasm. "That settles it! A bigger house!"

Amelia giggled delightedly and then stopped still. "But Maurie... what if you can't?"

"But I can. I have already. We will move out to Redwood Park. Big house. It already has a library... we can add my books to it. It has a big yard. Big trees for swings and cubby houses. All the things children need to grow. We will have a hundred children!"

"Redwood Park? Mrs Granger's Redwood Park?" She paled and felt a little dizzy and stood still hanging on to the back of the chair. "Oh Maurice. You said Mrs Granger... Bates... is a Benny. I don't think I could live with Mrs Gr... Bates again. I would be so scared. What if she was mean to our babies?" She glanced over at Zach and then paled a little more. "Oh, Zach, I am so sorry. I mean no disrespect. I know she is your sister."

Maurice held his fingers to his wife's lips and held her close. "Hush my dear Amelia. You won't have to live with Mrs Benny. I would never allow it! Just us and a housemaid or two if we can find any who will hire out. Not many of them around these days."

"Really? Mrs Granger... Mr and Mrs Bates... will not be there?"

Zach spoke up. "Bates has already gone. Heather is leaving. An unsupported lifestyle is not to her liking."

Maurice gently tried to allay her fears. "I know it is not ideal — not having the house staff that place is used to. But we have put our heads together and come up with some ideas."

"Ideas...?" Tibby stood at the door holding Millie on her hip.

Bailey deferred to Zach as Tibby walked back inside. "Like... hiring out the Redwood huts to travellers."

Bailey smiled indulgently at Amelia and patted her belly. "Gold-diggers aren't known for paying for legal services unless they've got a noose around their neck. With this rush I need something more than lawyering to support our family."

"Oh Maurie, I am relieved. I thought you meant you would be following them out to the goldfields. I am so very glad..."

"With a baby on the way? No! But we're all keen to get our hands on some of that gold, but we are thinking more in line with this. Zach and Tacko will be our partners."

Zach shifted his weight. "Redwood Park is on the main road since they opened the Gilyard Range pass. It would make an ideal way-station going out to the goldfields. We could sell gear and rations that prospectors need to set themselves up. The sheds and workshops at Redwood have already been pilfered of anything remotely useful that is not nailed down. Miners need gear, so we might as well provide it at a price, rather than it sitting there for them to pinch."

Tibby jiggled Millie on her hip. "I thought you told Heather we would not move to Redwood."

"Not us. Bailey and Amelia. They will manage it as 'Redwood Inn'. Tacko and Hilda will set up the Smithy's Shed to forge tools and other jobs on commission. We will expand the garden so we can supply meals. The dam wall is coming down. As soon as it rains, the lagoon will refill. The gold won't last forever, but this may be what gets us through."

Tibby smiled, looking around the group that she now called family. Hilda put a loaf of bread on the table with some salted beef.

Tacko thumped Bailey on the shoulder and took up the knife and began to saw some slices. Amelia came and took Millie from her arms, dancing around the room whispering secrets of a coming playmate. Tibby was quietly amazed. How could she have ever conceived that this would be the destination of the journey she started that day when she walked up the gang-plank with a ticket and a dream and a laugh on her lips? How she wanted to thank that smiling naïve child of a woman for courageously stepping out towards her future in faith. She was grateful that girl started this journey because it had brought her here.

She realised then, that just like the Bible story, the enemy had left in the night and abandoned their tents. God *had* intervened for them! She expected there would be other times on their journey where they would see his grace. This felt like they had paused to rest at a wayside inn: a place of comfort and refreshment; companionship and grace. Oh yes, she was grateful... and, just as Dellaweir had been those things for her, her prayer was that this next season would also be that for other travellers down the track.

And it was.

Coming soon from Olwyn Harris: Pioneers of Grace Series

Book 4 - Mask of Grace

Late one night, Martha finds herself at a wayside inn, running from the expectations of her family. To stay in hiding, she works as a scullery maid alongside Simmons, who doesn't just cook, but is a culinary artist. Intrigued by each other's secrets, will they be able to drop their pretence long enough to find their true passions?

Book 5 – Crucible of Grace

Ruth has had more than her fair share of tragedy. When her widowed mother-in-law wants to return to the farming region where her family once thrived, Ruth works as a laundry maid to support them. Can Ruth survive the fire of heartache and prejudice to find a new shape for her life, which might even include the station owner?

Book 6 – Sculpture of Grace

Rachel loves her country life. She loves her art of forging iron and her growing friendship with the station's newest blacksmith. Leah, her older sister, on the other hand, does not like anything country. But, as fate would have it, Rachel is offered a proposal which means she would have to leave the valley she loves, while Leah is sidelined and mourns her dreams of more. Can the sisters find a way to reconcile their destinies and forge a different story where they both see their dreams come true?

More Books by this Author

Pioneers of Grace Series

Book 1 - Time of Grace

Abigail is the elegant wife of the most powerful station-owner in the valley. But powerful also means brutish and cruel. To correct her husband's crimes, Abby is drawn into contact with the disgraced lawyer Ruben Davey, hiding in the hills with a band of displaced bushrangers. Will Abby be able to address these injustices and find a way to navigate towards a safer future in the meantime?

Book 2 - Circle of Grace

All her life Hannah had been sensible and sincere. When her humble circumstances lead her to work as the companion for Lady Whitmore, she is confronted with Lady Whitmore's nephew, the most shallow and irresponsible man she has ever met. As their life of privilege collapses around them, will she follow Lady Whitmore and Sebastian to Australia, to explore a new life in exile?

#1 The Beachside Cottage

In this offering from Olwyn Harris, we meet the heartbroken and downtrodden Eliza-Beth Perkins. Eliza-Beth is facing the dire consequences of her choices and the possibility of life in the poorhouse. Then she, literally, runs into Jensen Harker. Jensen is facing his own heartbreak at the death of his wife and wants nothing more than to be left alone. But something in Eliza-Beth stirs him to make a rash proposal, thus rescuing her from her predicament. As we follow their journey together, will we see them find the healing they both desperately need?

#2 Petrea Downs

In the 2nd book in this series, we meet Meg. Meg's life has been turned upside-down, with her husband gone, trying to run Petrea Downs by herself, and disaster after disaster at every turn. Thankfully, her neighbour Everett Grossman is always there to help. The final blow comes when a cattle duffer tries to steal her only source of income, gets shot, and has to be nursed back to  health in her living room. But, is Ben Harker really the villain he seems? And is Everett really the hero he makes himself out to be?

#3 The Writer's Retreat

The third book in the Homes of Healing trilogy introduces us to Tess, a romance writer, who prides herself on letting her characters tell their own story. When she arrives at Rocky Creek B&B, the run-down stone cottage looks like the perfect place for her to retreat to, not only to write her book, but to escape her past. Join her as she discovers her characters and explores their stories, and finds that God is intent on becoming part of her own story at the same time. As her relationship with the local publican challenges her to stop running, she realises that real life and real love can be messy and complicated. Can she honestly confront the ugly aspects in her own story, so that God can bring them both to a place of healing?

#1 Sapphires of Hope

"There is no way," she thought, "that I am going to use this!" She had desperately searched their cupboards for something, anything that would come close to what she needed for her catering project. She found only this old dilapidated breadbasket that looked like the sort of junk that comes from one of those tacky jumble-sale stalls..."

Andi and Jo are best friends... they do pretty much everything together. So, when Andi has a catering assignment due, and only a tacky old basket to use, Jo helps her pull off the faded decorations, revealing a time-capsule of historical information, and in order to understand what it means, Andi and Jo ask their elderly neighbour to take them to visit the farm where the basket came from. They find themselves dumped back in history at the time of Federation, embroiled in circumstances that nearly cost Andi her life and threatens the livelihood of the people living there. How can they ever hope to keep going when things are spinning out of control?

#2 Rubies of Ambition

In the 2nd book in the Gem of Australia series, we again travel with Andi and Jo back in time. On this adventure, they meet the very beautiful and ambitious actress, Lillian Browning, who is on the run from the federal police. Andi and Jo accompany her back to her hometown, where they find she is not well received. Will Lillian find a balance between the past that calls her and the ambitions that drive her?

#3 Emerald Dreams

In the third instalment of the *Gems of Australia* series, Olwyn Harris brings Australian history to life as she takes us on a journey back to the early days of convict settlement in Australia. Here we, once again, find Andi and Jo learning about Australia's true history, and finding strength in God to help others.

#1: A Spacious Place

In this first instalment of the Guthrie's Lot series, set in the late 1800s, we meet Irvin Guthrie, a practical, no-nonsense man with a sick wife and a small child to care for. When his wife's doctor suggests they move to a warmer climate, he spends everything he has on a property that ends up not being what he expected.

Joanna Grenham has dreams of being a schoolteacher. When an opportunity presents itself, she jumps at the chance, only to find herself given no choice but to care for Irvin's sick wife and child.

Will Irvin and Joanna make the most of their circumstances, or will they forever find life as hard and unyielding as the ground in A Spacious Place.

#2: A Level Path

In the second instalment of the Guthrie's Lot series, it is now the late 1960s. Here we meet Irvin's granddaughter Iris. Iris hungers for excitement and adventure, and she won't find that in Gumleigh, or with the ever-predictable Dave. The last thing she expected was for Dave to follow her across the world to England as she tries to find direction and meaning.

Will Iris finally see through the charismatic, but ultimately selfish, Stan, or will Dave leave England alone and leave Iris to find her own way to A Level Path?

#3: The Crying Tree

In this final episode of the Guthrie's Lot series, the year is now 2010. We meet Mac, who has always been an achiever – a do-er, just like her father. After the death of her mother, she finds that she needs to get away, so she buys a little run-down stone cottage in the middle of nowhere to transform into a creative studio. She is taken by the feel of the place - especially the twisted weeping willow tree behind the house, even though it doesn't fit into her plans anywhere.

Dan spent years growing up on the old Guthrie place, so when the new owner arrives, he is not convinced that he wants to work for this headstrong woman, who is obviously used to getting what she wants, but he feels that it is something he has to do – and only God knows why.

Can Dan and Mac work together to make her dreams into a reality? Will she transform the old Guthrie place, and her life, into something unique and beautiful? And what will become of The Crying Tree.

Matt's Boys of Wattle Creek

When Matthew Lawson's three sons were born, he wrote each of them a letter outlining his hopes and prayers for their futures. When he decided to give up his city job and move to the little town of Wattle Creek, he could never have imagined the effect it would have on his young family. As Matt's boys grow to maturity and find their places in their community, will his dreams and prayers come to fulfilment? Will his boys develop their own faith in the eternal God? And will they each find the kind of love that Matt holds for his beautiful Josie?

Maggie & Minotaur

"For Maggie, the mythical Minotaur represented Romance – half man, half beast. The Minotaur was a monster created from centuries of classical Greek mythology and no normal man could withstand its strength...... Sooner or later she would accept that Theseus, the hero, did not exist. She knew that she would have to battle through the maze of reality and confront it herself...."

Maggie Wick was shipped off to the city and high society life at the age of 12, where she would learn the ways of the rich and marry into a family of influence. What could have caused her sudden return to Henderson's Gap? Can she really settle back into life on the station, with all its diversity and challenges? Will she find fulfilment in her role as provisional schoolteacher? Will she ever figure out the "Captain", the mysterious, intimidating, station manager? When war comes to her little haven and Maggie's world comes crashing down, taking her loved ones and the captain with it, Maggie needs to find a way to survive. Will her faith be enough to protect her, and what of the Captain? Could he really be the Theseus who would do battle with her Minotaur?

The Bush Olympics

The Bush Olympics, written by Olwyn Harris and beautifully illustrated by Shelly Askew, shows us that we don't have to be good at everything to be part of a team. Even sleepy Koala is good at something, and if everyone plays their part, we can all be successful together.